E

'An impressionable virgin' Lyle had called
Sarah when he interviewed her for a job
on his newspaper in the Caribbean—a
mockingly accurate assessment which
promptly made Sarah determined to
become a woman of the world. And who
better to teach her than Lyle himself? But
then, too late, Sarah's courage began to
fail her . . .

BLUE DAYS
AT SEA

BY

ANNE WEALE

MILLS & BOON LIMITED

15-16 BROOK'S MEWS
LONDON W1A 1DR

First published 1981
Australian copyright 1981
Philippine copyright 1981
This edition 1981

© Anne Weale 1981

ISBN 0 263 73649 0

Set in Monophoto Baskerville 10 on 11 pt.

Made and printed in Great Britain by
Richard Clay (The Chaucer Press) Ltd,
Bungay, Suffolk

I will make you brooches and toys for your delight
Of bird-song at morning and star-shine at night.
I will make a palace fit for you and me
Of green days in forests and blue days at sea.

Robert Louis Stevenson

CHAPTER ONE

SARAH GRAHAM had not told her parents about the interview. They had tickets for the theatre that evening, and
were giving her a lift into central London. When her
mother had asked where she was going, Sarah had said,
'I'm meeting Liz,' which was true.

She *was* meeting her friend, but not until after the interview at the Westbury Hotel.

Sitting in the back of her father's comfortable Rover—
her mother had a smaller car for shopping which Sarah
sometimes used in the evening, but at present it was under
repair—she wondered what her parents would think if they
did know about the interview. She was sure her father
would disapprove, as he had disapproved of but not ac-
tively opposed her decision to become a journalist instead
of following in his footsteps.

John Graham was a successful solicitor with a practice in
a part of London where there was a large West Indian
community. He had been born in the West Indies, in the
days before those of the islands which formerly had been
governed by Britain had won their independence.

During the past twenty-five years, as the number of
islanders leaving the Caribbean to come and work in
England had increased, so had his reputation for being a
trustworthy lawyer who understood West Indians, their
background, their difficulties, their vulnerability to un-
scrupulous landlords, even the dialects which, when they
were worried and upset, made the English of new arrivals
as incomprehensible to the average Londoner as a strong
Irish brogue or a heavy Scots accent.

John Graham had been to school in England, and had

7

gone on to become a brilliant undergraduate at Cambridge. But his boyhood holidays had been spent on an island in the Leeward group and he could, on occasion, lapse into the vernacular of his youth. He would still be speaking English, but in a form which his wife could not understand except for a word here and there, although his daughter could follow most of it.

Looking at the back of his head, Sarah was reasonably confident that he would not oppose her latest venture—if it came off.

She knew her mother would be extremely distressed at the idea of her leaving home. There was no point in worrying either of them about something which might never happen.

The Grahams had hoped to have several children, but had had to be content with one daughter. She loved them as dearly as they loved her, but sometimes she felt a little smothered by their protectiveness, and recently her mother had been fostering the courtship of a young man whom Sarah liked but had no wish to marry.

Her application for the job advertised in the World's Press News had been partly a bid for greater freedom. Her other motive had been an almost lifelong desire to see the island which had lured her ever since, when she was a little girl, her father had made his boyhood escapades into bedtime stories for her.

'We have time to drop Sarah at Liz's flat, haven't we, John?' said her mother. 'I don't like her walking about on her own at night. One hears of such terrible things happening.'

'Not at this time of night, or in the area where Liz lives,' said Sarah, from the back seat. 'Drop me at the end of Bond Street, would you, please, Dad? It's late opening tonight, so Liz will be working until eight. I want to look in the shop windows before I meet her. I shan't get mugged in Bond

Street, darling,' she added, leaning forward to give her mother a reassuring pat on the shoulder.

Alike in looks, they were utterly dissimilar in temperament. Mrs Graham always foresaw every possible snag and disaster. Sarah was naturally optimistic, although her usual sunny self-confidence was not in operation as far as the coming interview was concerned.

She felt there were bound to be many other applicants for such a plum of an opportunity, and her qualifications, although good for her age, were necessarily more limited than those of an older applicant.

'Thanks, Dad. See you later, Mother. Enjoy yourselves,' she said warmly, when they dropped her.

It was not far from the Piccadilly end of Bond Street to the corner of Conduit Street and the hotel where she was being interviewed. The appointment had been arranged on the telephone with the secretary of the man who had advertised the job which Sarah wanted more than anything she had ever wanted in her life.

The advertisement was imprinted in her mind.

Caribbean weekly newspaper, COMPOSTELA INDEPENDENT, *requires fully trained woman journalist, aged 25–35, for general reporting and women's features.*

The shop windows which were not lighted reflected her in their dark panes as she hurried past; a slim girl with long, slender legs and a head-hugging cap of small dark curls which emphasised the shape of her head and its poise on her graceful neck.

She had not dressed up for the interview, but was wearing her usual working clothes; a loose off-white raincoat, regularly cleaned, over a pleated wool skirt in a grey and black plaid with a thread of pink in it, this colour picked up by a pale pink shirt underneath a deep rose pink sweater. Well-polished black leather shoes with heels made for comfortable walking, a capacious black shoulder bag, and a

Jaeger silk scarf completed an outfit which would take her from a morning reporting the proceedings in the borough magistrates' court to a midday assignment to cover a luncheon club meeting, or an evening taking notes at the A.G.M. of one of the local organisations.

Some girls of her age might have been shy of walking into the luxurious lounge-foyer of a West End hotel. But Sarah was a born journalist; much too interested in her surroundings and in the people she met ever to suffer the nervous shrinking of a more self-absorbed type of girl. It never worried her that people might not like her, because she found them so interesting. Everyone, however dull they might seem on first acquaintance, had *something* noteworthy about them.

'Good evening.' Her lips parted to show the perfect teeth which she considered her only beauty as she smiled at one of the men behind the hall porters' desk. 'I have an appointment with Mr L. R. Talbot. Could you tell me where I shall find him, please?'

The porter told her where to go, and indicated the lifts. Sarah thanked him and walked towards them. A party of people in evening dress were stepping out of the lift on the right, and her observant tawny eyes took in the details of the women's dresses and their furs and jewels as they passed her.

Her mother had wanted her to have a fox jacket for her recent twenty-first birthday. But although she liked clothes Sarah had felt that an expensive fur would be wasted on her. Instead she had persuaded her parents to buy her a Persian rug which would give her pleasure every day of her life, now and in the future when she married and had a home of her own. Not that she wanted to marry until she was at least twenty-five, possibly thirty. She had many ambitions to fulfil before she would be ready to settle down.

She and the liftman were alone as he took her up to the floor she wanted. Knowing that not much escaped hotel staff, she asked, 'Has Mr Talbot interviewed a lot of people today?'

'Yes, a good many, miss. One about every half hour since I came on duty at three.'

Her spirits sank. It didn't sound promising, especially as she was four years outside the age range given in the advertisement. She had carefully avoided mentioning her age in the curriculum vitae she had sent in reply, but it was certain to come out during the interview.

'Good luck, miss,' the liftman said, as she stepped into a thickly-carpeted corridor.

She flashed her wide smile at him. But as she advanced along the corridor, looking for the right number, some unaccustomed butterflies began to flutter inside her. Being interviewed by a prospective employer was very different from interviewing someone for her paper.

Mr L. R. Talbot did not keep her waiting for more than a few moments before he opened the door to her. Her eyes widened as she looked at him. Because the Westbury was part of an American chain of hotels, much patronised by American visitors to London, she had jumped to the conclusion that he would be an American.

He was not: nor was he a stranger. She had seen him before, many times.

His face was well-known to anyone who watched BBC Television. As Lyle Talbot, he was one of the British Broadcasting Corporation's most accomplished roving reporters. Moreover, he had begun his career as a newspaper reporter, and on the very same suburban London paper on which she worked.

'Good evening, Miss Graham. Please come in.' He opened the door to its fullest extent, and stood back for her to enter the lobby of his suite. He had left an inner door open, giving a glimpse of a comfortably appointed sitting-room.

'G-good evening.'

It was no longer pre-interview nerves which made Sarah stammer a little as she returned his greeting. Surprise had ousted trepidation—surprise mingled with dismay.

For although no one could dispute Lyle Talbot's brilliance and charm as a television journalist, what Sarah knew of his private persona made her think he must be a prize rat.

'May I take your coat?'

'Thank you.' She put her bag on a chair and unfastened the buttons of her raincoat. Even with a window open, the level of central heating was high. He helped her to withdraw her arms from the sleeves. While he laid the coat aside, she took off her scarf, folded it and put it inside her bag.

'Please sit down, Miss Graham.' He indicated the chair she should take. 'May I offer you something to drink?'

'No, thank you.'

'You don't drink, or you don't believe in mixing business and pleasure?'

She began to cross her legs, but checked the movement and kept her feet side by side.

'I do drink, although not very much, and not when I need all my wits about me,' she said lightly.

He laughed, and sat down on the sofa directly opposite her. It was difficult to judge a man's size from seeing him on television. The breadth of his shoulders had suggested that he was tall, but neither her editor nor Rosemary had ever mentioned that he was several inches above six feet; a lean-hipped, long-legged giant.

Sarah knew he must be about twelve years older than herself, but he wasn't beginning to go to seed as men sometimes did in their early thirties. There was no sign of Lyle Talbot's neck or midriff beginning to thicken. If she had seen him downstairs in the lobby and not known how he made his living, she would have taken him for an international-class sportsman. A tennis player or a cricketer, maybe, except that it was winter, the wrong time of year for such people to be in London.

He gave her a long, thoughtful scrutiny which might have unnerved her had she not been interested in comparing the face familiar from television with the real-life man seated a few yards away.

On the various occasions when she had seen other famous faces in the flesh, they had always been slightly disappointing; the charisma less potent in reality than on the large or small screen. But this was not the case with him. His magnetism seemed even stronger. She had never met a more attractive man. Even if she had not been told that he used his attractiveness with a complete lack of scruple where women were concerned, she would have been wary of responding to it.

Accustomed to taking the initiative in interviews, and forgetting that her role this time should be passive, she said, 'I don't understand your connection with the *Compostela Independent*, Mr Talbot. How can you edit the paper when you're busy with your television assignments?'

'I'm giving up working for television. It was only a means to an end. I prefer newspaper journalism.'

'Really?' she said, in astonishment.

She would have supposed that the running of a small weekly paper would seem very tame compared with jetting round the world to the latest trouble spots.

'That surprises you,' was his comment. 'At your age, it would have surprised me. How old are you, Miss Graham? Not twenty-five, by the look of you.'

'No . . . no, not quite,' she admitted.

He tilted an eyebrow. 'I hope you're not usually vague. You can't be, or Bob wouldn't keep you.'

This was a reference to her present editor.

'I'll be twenty-two on my next birthday.'

A glint of humour lit his dark brown eyes. He had thick, wiry hair like her father, and his haircut was as conventional as her father's. But whereas Mr Graham's hair had been greying for ten years or more, and his chin was clean-shaven, Lyle Talbot's hair was still black.

'A date you omitted to mention in your letter,' he remarked dryly.

He took from the table at his elbow a sheaf of correspondence attached to a clipboard. As he moved it, Sarah recognised the uppermost letter as hers.

'The tenth of November,' she told him.

'So you're only just twenty-one?'

'Yes, but is there a special reason why the successful applicant must be three years and nine months older than I am?'

'I usually have reasons for my actions,' was his somewhat caustic reply.

Sarah felt her assurance ebbing. 'Would you mind explaining the reason for that particular proviso?'

'I didn't think anyone under twenty-five would be sufficiently experienced, either professionally or in their private life, to qualify for a place in my team. It will be very much a team job, reviving the old *Compostela News* in the form of the new *Independent*. If it hadn't been for Bob singing your praises to me, you wouldn't be here now, Miss Graham. I should have turned you down without seeing you, as I did about a dozen other applicants whose letters were unsatisfactory.'

'You mean Bob knows I've applied?' she asked, in some dismay.

'No, he doesn't. But he knows about my plans, and that I was behind the advertisement. I have dinner with him and Maggie every so often, and the last time we ate together I discussed the staff I was going to need. He mentioned you as an ideal candidate—in some ways.'

'But not in others?' she queried.

Again the glint lit his eyes. 'Now you're itching to know how he described you.'

'Naturally. Who wouldn't be?'

'All right, I'll tell you. He said you were an extremely intelligent, nice young woman, and an efficient, reliable journalist in all the ways required of a girl on an otherwise all-male staff. He couldn't have praised you more highly.' He paused. 'But he said you wouldn't do for my staff, so I needn't be tempted to try to induce you to leave him.'

'Why wouldn't I do?'

'Too young, and by far too innocent to be whisked off across the Atlantic and exposed to all the dubious influences on an island which is, among other things, a playground for the very rich. You still live at home with your parents, I believe?'

'Yes, I do,' she conceded. 'But no one who has clocked up as many hours of court-reporting as I have is ignorant of the seamy side of life, Mr Talbot. On that count I know a good deal more about life than my mother who is forty-four.'

'But no longer an impressionable virgin'—was his sardonic riposte.

He was beginning to fluster her. 'W-what do you mean by that?'

'Bob and Mary think that as well as being a nice girl in the general sense of being good-humoured and unselfish, you are also a girl who has yet to have her first lover. To people of their generation, it's a point in your favour. From my point of view it's a disadvantage.'

At this Sarah's firm chin lifted. 'I thought you wanted a competent girl reporter. If there would be extraneous duties, I'm afraid I'm not interested, Mr Talbot. I won't waste any more of your time, or my time.'

She jumped to her feet and moved to snatch up her raincoat.

'Stop flapping and sit down, Miss Graham.'

His voice was quiet, but there was a ring of authority in it which made her hesitate long enough for him to add,

'There would be no extraneous duties of the kind you appear to have in mind. Your condition—which you have confirmed by jumping to the wrong conclusion, and panicking—is a disadvantage because I need a girl reporter who won't lose her heart or her head, as virgins are apt to do until they acquire some wisdom. I shall have more pressing preoccupations than to keep a fatherly eye on you when the local wolves start to prowl. As, inevitably, they will—black and white.'

She was still on her feet. His dark gaze travelled slowly downwards from her face to her neatly shod feet and back to her face. 'You're an attractive girl. Bob and Mary neglected to mention how attractive, or I shouldn't have asked you to come here.'

'I don't know why you did ask me, as I seem to have everything against me—except my professional abilities.' Having no hope of the job now, she allowed herself a tinge of sarcasm.

'But one thing so much in your favour that it might yet outweigh all the cons,' was his unexpected response. 'None of the other applicants has any connection with the Caribbean in general or this island in particular. You have. Your father was born there, and being the daughter of John Graham gives you an entrée. In any small, tight community an entrée can be extremely important, if not essential.'

He rose and picked up the glass which, since she had entered the room, had stood empty on the glass-topped end table beside the arm of the sofa.

'You state in your letter that you know a great deal about the island in spite of never having been there,' he said, as he crossed the room to open a cupboard containing drinks. 'Does that mean your parents never go back?'

'No, never. My father loved the island as a boy, but it doesn't appeal to him now, or to my mother. His interests are music and painting and ancient history. They go to places like Florence and Delphi for their holidays, or to visit my grandparents in Scotland. They're my mother's people. My other grandparents are dead.'

'So apart from what he hears from his clients, your father has no direct experience of the changes which have taken place since the island became self-governing, apart from continuing its association with Britain in matters of defence policy?'

'No,' she agreed, watching him come towards her with a glass of sherry.

'I don't think this is likely to scatter your wits, but it may help smooth your ruffled feathers, Miss Graham,' he said with a lurking twinkle.

'Thank you.'

As she took it from him, she noticed his long, lean fingers and neatly trimmed, well-scrubbed nails. His hands looked stronger and more sinewy than those of most journalists; as if they were sometimes used for tasks requiring more muscle than typing or, in his case, recording a report.

'When your father lived on the island, the most exclusive section of island society was made up of white people— Creole planters and Colonial Service administrators and their families,' he explained, as he poured his own drink. 'At that time the majority of black people were still illiterate labourers, most of them not much better off than in the days of slavery. There was then a small middle class which today has expanded enormously, while the white élite has gone for ever, and illiteracy is on the way out as the older people, who had no proper schooling, die.'

He returned to the sofa and sat down.

'Thirty years ago, the only woman reporter who would have been acceptable to the white wives, with their servants and their dinner party rivalry, would have had to be white and well connected. Now the pendulum has swung in the other direction, and although the educated West Indian abhors irrational prejudice as much as any civilised person, there are those who make the past an excuse for perpetuating racial animosity.'

He drew up a silk-socked ankle and rested it on the knee of his other leg in the posture of a man at ease both physically and mentally. Sarah wished she felt equally relaxed.

'The island's economy is now as heavily dependent on tourism as it once was on sugar,' he went on, 'and yet you will meet a few tourists who have been subjected to hostility merely because they have white skins. In my book anti-white hatred is as stupid as anti-black hatred. But you can't ignore its existence. Most of the candidates for this job know nothing about the West Indies or their inhabitants. You do, and furthermore your surname is known to and respected by many Compostelans in London and, by report, to their friends and relations on the island. That's a very important pro to balance against several cons, Miss Graham.'

'The main con being my lack of . . . worldly experience.'

He nodded. 'That is so.'

She fixed her large amber eyes—said to be an inheritance from her French great-grandmother—on his face, and said levelly, 'That kind of experience is very easy to come by, and quite hard to avoid, Mr Talbot. You described me just now as attractive. I work with men and among men. Reporters . . . police officers . . . defending solicitors . . . secretaries of sports clubs . . . all kinds of men of all ages. It's not boasting to say that if I didn't have any evening assignments, I could have a date every night. So could any passable girl reporter. Don't you think the fact that I haven't yet had any lovers indicates that, far from being liable to lose my head, I have it screwed on very firmly?'

'It's a point with some force,' he said, smiling. 'I'll bear it in mind.'

This sounded a little more promising. She said, 'Would you mind if I asked you a question?'

'Go ahead.'

'What is your connection with the West Indies?'

'Like yours, my father was born there. He was an engineer who enlisted in the Royal Air Force at the outset of the Second World War, and stayed on here for a few years afterwards. I was born in Britain, and brought up all over the world, wherever my father's work took us. It was sailing—my relaxation—which eventually led me to the Leeward Islands. It surprised me to find no newspaper in Compostela. I felt it was a bad thing at a time when, throughout the Caribbean, people are being influenced by Cuba and Third World countries where there is strong Communist pressure. The lack of a free, responsible newspaper is extremely dangerous to free speech and informed opinions. It seemed a worthwhile undertaking to re-establish a paper in Compostela and perhaps, later on, to revive the *Star* in Antigua.'

He took up the clipboard again, his glance swiftly scanning her letter.

'Kew Green. A nice place to live—very different from the district where you work. What kind of living conditions do you envisage if you came to work in Compostela?'

'A room with a local family would be the best thing, I should think. Or does everyone cater to tourists, making ordinary digs hard to come by?'

'No, we could find you some digs—but they wouldn't be up to the standard of your parents' home at Kew. At times the island has serious water and power problems which can make life uncomfortable.'

'There's always the sea to cool off in if the shower runs dry, isn't there?'

'Yes, there's always the sea,' he agreed. 'Are you a swimmer?'

Sarah shook her head. 'Not a good one. I once managed a quarter of a mile in the pool at school, and I passed the life-saving test. But I've done very little sea-swimming.'

'You haven't asked me about the salary. Or does a parental subsidy make that unimportant?' he asked.

'I don't know why you assume that, because my father is successful, I must be thoroughly pampered,' was her indignant reply. 'Can you really see a spoilt little rich girl working on the *News*, Mr Talbot? I may live at home, but I've always contributed something towards my keep. Probably my parents bank it, and will give it back to me eventually. They don't need my contribution, but my father thinks it wrong, on principle, to allow a grown-up daughter to fritter every penny she earns. As it happens, I fritter very little. In my job, the latest fashions would look ridiculous. My only extravagance is books.'

'Mine, too.' He was looking amused again. 'You needn't have flared up, Miss Graham. I wasn't implying that you were spoilt. If I were in the habit of pre-judging people, Bob and Maggie would have disabused me of that idea. Is your temper always so combustible?'

Aware that she had reacted with rather more fire than was proper in an interviewee, Sarah shifted uncomfortably.

'I'm sorry. You're right,' she apologised. 'I don't often flare up like that. I suppose I'm more keyed up than usual. I—I want this job very much, and it's frustrating to feel that I have the right qualifications except for being slightly under the age range and . . . and never having slept with anyone,' she added, a shade bitterly.

'But you do know how to apologise, which is more than can be said of everyone.' He rose to his feet. 'Thank you for coming, Miss Graham. I was inclined to think Bob and his wife had overrated you. I was mistaken. But whether or not you are the right girl for my newspaper is something I shall have to ponder. Either way, I will let you know as soon as possible.'

He was walking to the door as he spoke.

'Did you come by car or by Underground?'

'I was given a lift. Now I'm going out to supper with a friend.'

'One of all those men you're surrounded by?'

'No, a girl—a school friend.'

'If my ears burn later this evening, I shall know why,' he said dryly, stepping past her to open the outer door.

In the confined space of the lobby he seemed even taller and broader. Sarah was not a short girl, but he dwarfed her. Yet his handclasp though strong was not painful as his fingers closed over hers.

'Goodnight, Mr Talbot.'

'Goodnight, Sarah Graham.'

She knew that he watched her walk part of the way along the corridor because she had gone several yards before she heard the door close behind her.

'Got the job, miss?' the liftman enquired.

'I don't know yet. It's a case of "Don't call us, we'll call you,"' she told him.

Downstairs, between the two pairs of glass doors which protected the foyer from draughts, she put on her raincoat and checked the time.

She had been upstairs twenty minutes. Perhaps, as she walked away, another candidate would arrive. Or perhaps she had been the last one, and the rest of his evening was free for the current woman in his life. She felt sure there was one. Or, if he was only in London temporarily, having already moved his belongings to Compostela, an old flame whom he could look up.

Not Rosemary. She was married now, with two children. Her youthful affair with him was merely an unhappy memory which most of the time didn't trouble her. It was only when she saw him on television that she felt a twinge of the old pain, not because she loved him any more, but because of his shabby treatment of her.

Do I, in fact, want to work for him? Sarah asked herself,

as she hurried in the direction of Oxford Street. The answer was, Yes, more than ever, and she knew why.

Years ago, in her romantic mid-teens, she had fallen in love with Lyle Talbot in the way most girls of that age made idols of unattainable men.

Liz's heart-throb had been Robert Redford, but she had stopped mooning over him as soon as her parents had allowed her to start making live dates. Sarah's emotional adolescence had gone on longer. She had continued to daydream about Lyle after going out with several young men, none of whom had come up to his standard.

Her infatuation with his image had lasted right up to the night when Rosemary, the wife of one of the more senior *News* reporters, had told her the kind of person he really was.

It had been a shattering disillusionment to learn that her dream man was only a figment of her imagination; an impossibly perfect being grafted on to an image on the screen.

Now, with a sinking of the heart, she knew that his jibe about her being 'an impressionable virgin' was not without truth. She had thought she was grown-up, mature, a self-possessed, rational young career woman. But the truth—and she had to face it—was that from the moment she had entered his suite, the old magic had begun to work again. Physically, he was still her ideal, the only face she could imagine bending over her in the rapturous moment which she had so often imagined, but never experienced.

Elizabeth Brett was waiting outside the staff entrance of the department store where she was secretary to the managing director's deputy. It was a good post which she had achieved by being the star pupil of her year at one of the best secretarial training colleges. To Sarah, her friend's job sounded unbearably monotonous compared with the almost infinite variety of a reporter's work. But Liz seemed happy enough, and the difference in their temperaments had not prevented them from making friends at the age of twelve and remaining friends nine years later.

They met for supper at least once a fortnight, and were deeply in each other's confidence. Although Sarah had never had as much to confide as Liz who had left the parental nest at the age of eighteen, first to share a flat with another girl, and then with the man who had been the first of her two lovers.

At present her love life was in the doldrums after she had ended a relationship with a man she had discovered to be married.

Liz, as much of a realist as Sarah was a romantic, had seen too many other women held in cruel suspense by a lover who had no intention of breaking up a dull but comfortable marriage to endure the same torment herself. But the break had left her in low spirits.

The last time they had met she had said, in her flippant way, 'The trouble with men is they're addictive. Giving up sex is worse than giving up smoking. I'm beginning to wish I were like you—saving myself for Mr Right. If he exists.'

She already knew about the interview. Her first question, on seeing Sarah, was, 'How did it go?'

'Badly—in more ways than one. I knew my age would be against me, but I didn't bargain for the editor turning out to be Lyle Talbot.'

'You're not serious?' Liz knew about Sarah's teenage dream love. 'So you've met him at last. What was he like?'

By the time they had walked to an Italian restaurant round the corner from Liz's small flat, Sarah had related the details of the interview.

'Supposing you do get the job? Will you take it, now you know who you'll be working for?' asked Liz, when they had made their choice from the menu, and the waiter had filled their glasses from a carafe of the house wine.

'I don't know. I'll have to think about it. But I'm sure I

shan't get it,' said Sarah, tracing the checks on the red and white gingham tablecloth with the tip of a forefinger.

Her nails were painted with a lacquer to match her pink skirt, and she wore a variety of rings, none expensive but all unusual. On the little finger of her left hand was a silver ring, bought in Greece, fashioned in the shape of two rams' heads, their curly horns butting. On the little finger of her other hand was an antique flower ring set with stones as blue as the petals of a forget-me-not.

'If you do, I think you should take it,' remarked Liz. 'Although you said Rosemary put you off him when she told you how he let her down, I don't think we ever learn from other people's bad experiences.'

'You did with George,' Sarah reminded her. 'You stopped knowing him for precisely that reason—that you'd seen other people's disasters.'

'Yes, but I'm by nature a cynic, and you're an idealist,' said Liz. 'You've been crazy about Lyle Talbot since he first appeared on TV when you were thirteen or fourteen. It's my belief you still are. If that isn't so, why has no other man really made any serious impact with you?'

'I don't know,' said Sarah, with a shrug.

'For the simple reason that none of them matches up to *him*. That's why, sweetie. The only way you're going to get the man out of your system properly is by finding out at first hand that his charm is no more than skin deep. Otherwise there's a very good chance that, to use his phrase, you'll still be an impressionable virgin five years from now.'

'Last time we met you said you wished you were.'

'I do, and I don't,' said Liz, sighing. 'I see now that it was largely curiosity that made me got to bed with Peter— and very disappointing it was. He was nice, but not as a lover. George was great, but there was no future in it. At least when the next man comes along, I shan't have my judgment warped by impatience to know what it's all about. I——'

She was interrupted by the arrival of their *agnello al forno*, a dish of lamb flavoured with rosemary and garlic, and cooked in wine with potatoes and button mushrooms. With crusty bread and a side salad, it was one of their favourite meals, and they had tried all the small restaurants in the village-like network of streets surrounding Liz's flat.

'What's the pay like? Better than what you get now?' she asked presently.

'I forgot to go into that,' Sarah admitted, rather sheepishly. 'He did bring up the subject, but in a way that made me annoyed—by implying I was a rich man's daughter merely playing at journalism. By the time I'd established that I wasn't, and apologised for jumping down his throat, I'd forgotten all about the pay. Soon after that he stood up and showed me out. Which suggests that he hadn't put me on his mental short-list,' she added wryly.

'Looking at it selfishly, the last thing I want is for you to shoot off abroad,' said Liz. 'I should miss you tremendously, Sarah—especially now, while there isn't a man in my life. But I do think, from your point of view, it's time to break the apron-strings. Your mother is a dear. I envy your relationship with her, having nothing but rows with my own mama. But obviously yours is determined to see you married to one of her friends' sons, preferably the eligible Roddy, and how much longer can you resist her coercion?'

'It is tricky,' Sarah admitted. 'I'm going out with him tomorrow night. There was just no way to avoid it and, in a way, I didn't want to. He's nice. I like him. It's going to be a super party. If only I wasn't afraid of his getting serious about me.'

'It could be that your indifference to him is the very thing to make him serious. It brings out the hunter in a man—an instinct which doesn't have so much scope in these days when we're easier prey, not to say sitting ducks.'

Sarah said, 'So far he hasn't even kissed me, which is odd, because other girls say he's the world champion pouncer.'

'A bad sign, that. I know of only two reasons why a man on a date doesn't try even a tentative pounce. Either he's gone off the idea, and the first date is also the last. Or, for a reason which isn't immediately clear to him, he wants this girl to be different. If he pounces, and she responds with too much enthusiasm, he's actually going to be disappointed. Love still makes some men amazingly old-fashioned. It's fine, us all being madly liberated while a man only wants a no-strings romp. But love seems to revive his possessive feelings.'

'Yes, that's what I've noticed,' said Sarah. 'Which makes Roddy's behaviour rather ominous. I don't want to hurt him.'

'If I were in your shoes, I'd think twice about turning down a man with as much to offer as Roddy has. Yes, I know you think love is the vital thing. But is it really, in the long run? When the kissing has to stop—or at least to become less exciting—it must be a help to have other forms of excitement to fall back on. Gorgeous clothes, a lovely house, glamorous holidays, extravagant Christmas and birthday presents.'

'I don't believe the kissing does have to stop,' was Sarah's firm answer. 'I was reading a review of a book called *The Psychology of Romantic Love* the other day. The critic said that the author, Nathaniel Branden, championed the unfashionable view that a sexually exclusive romantic love relationship might be the most exciting adventure there is. That's for me. That's what I want from life.'

'Are you sure you couldn't have it with Roddy?'

'No, I could have a comfortable life just like my mother has, but I'm not ready for that. I want to spread my wings first. I haven't any real hope of going to work in

Compostela, but applying for that job has put me in the mood to try for others.'

The next morning Sarah arrived at the office before the rest of the editorial staff. The first thing she did after lighting the ancient gas fire in the shabby, desk-crowded reporters' room was to go to the editor's office and check the diary.

This was a large desk diary in which he wrote all the events which the paper would cover, and added to them the initials of the reporter best suited to each assignment. Sometimes there were last-minute additions to the list, and then the four staff reporters might be switched from one job to another. So checking the diary every morning was a vital part of her routine.

As it happened, today her initials were not against any of the entries, so she would be free—when not interrupted by the telephone—to work on the column for women which was her special responsibility.

The editor wrote the paper's leader column, the chief reporter wrote a collection of notes and comments of general interest, and another reporter compiled the sports notes.

As much as the variety of a reporter's work, Sarah liked the elasticity of the working hours. Because they often had to work in the evening, they were free during the day to go out for long, leisurely coffee breaks. They would take it in turns to stay to answer the telephone while the others walked round to the coffee shop to discuss the national and international news, or any other subject which came up.

By half past three the editor had read and approved her column.

He said, 'You might as well knock off now, Sarah.'

She went home, and took a long time having a warm, scented bath. She felt unusually tired. Normally she slept well, but last night she hadn't. Thoughts of the interview and of Lyle Talbot had kept her awake into the small hours.

When Roderick Benson's Datsun 280 ZX swept into the Graham's gravelled drive and drew up in front of their substantial Victorian family house, Sarah was waiting in the sitting-room. She was wearing a classic shirt-dress of vivid geranium red chiffon with high-heeled evening shoes to match. Round her neck hung a gold letter S, and her ear-rings were tiny gold butterflies.

Most of the daughters of her parents' friends had furs, or borrowed their mothers' when they went out at night. Sarah preferred to wear a short but snug quilted silk jacket. It was reversible; black on one side, red on the other.

She let Roddy in and he had a few words with her parents. He was wearing the latest thing in dinner jackets. The Bensons were more than slightly *nouveau riche* and always had the latest everything. Sarah suspected that her mother would have liked to emulate them but was restrained by her father, who enjoyed his success but did not feel the need to advertise it with a succession of costly acquisitions.

'You look very pretty tonight, Sarah,' said Roddy, turning to her.

He was three years her senior, but he didn't look twenty-four. Tonight he seemed even more boyish than usual compared with the tall, assured man whose face was still in the forefront of her mind.

She smiled. 'Thank you.' She had an intuitive feeling that he was disappointed by her plain, unrevealing dress.

His sisters were flamboyant dressers, and his other girl-friends had excellent figures and displayed them to the full. Probably he had hoped she would wear a sexy crêpe-de-chine shift with thin straps, no bra and a slit up one thigh, she thought, hastily lowering her lashes to hide the sudden sparkle of laughter in her eyes.

That was one of the main reasons why their mothers'

matchmaking was doomed to fail: the difference in their senses of humour.

Roddy often told jokes; endless, boring shaggy dog stories, and sometimes anecdotes so risqué they made her uncomfortable. But these were all jokes he had heard. He never made up funny things, or noticed things she found amusing. She felt sure that Lyle Talbot would. All the lines on his face had been laughter lines; the slight crinkles round his dark eyes, and the two deeper grooves down his cheeks.

Stop it, she told herself severely. For this was the trap she had fallen into once before; the dangerous delusion of attributing to him all the qualities of her ideal man.

Liz had been right, she thought. She had been crazy about him for years, and still was, in spite of Rosemary. It was he who had made her decide to become a journalist, long before the rest of the girls in her form had decided where their talents lay.

'We won't be late, Mrs Graham, and don't worry, I'll be very careful how much I drink.'

She shook off her thoughts in time to hear Roddy saying all the right mother-reassuring things.

'I never worry when Sarah is out with you, Roddy,' was her mother's benignant reply.

About five hours later, when his car was again parked in the Grahams' drive, but this time with all its lights out, Sarah remembered this remark. In the circumstances it made her laugh, and her laughter was a more effective deterrent to his excess of ardour than her efforts to free herself from a goodnight embrace which had, all at once, got out of hand.

Suddenly, after kissing her on the lips with acceptable gentleness, he had bypassed the various stages between a light kiss and a passionate one, and begun to embrace her with a fervour she could not return.

'What's funny?' He sounded annoyed.

'I was wondering if my parents had heard the car, and

were waiting for it to leave: my mother assuring my father that nice, well-behaved Roddy would never step out of line.'

'I haven't . . . or not very far. You know I'm crazy about you, Sarah. Your parents wouldn't mind us kissing—they must have felt this way themselves once. I'm not just making a pass. I want to marry you.'

'Oh, dear . . . no, don't . . . *please* . . . I'm sorry.' She was filled with remorse for allowing him to get to this stage. 'I'm not in love with you, Roddy.'

'But you like me a little bit, don't you?'

'Of course, but——' The rest was stifled as he forced another, more sensuous kiss on her.

This time she struggled vigorously and, when she could breathe, said, 'But I *don't* like being kissed like that.'

'God! You really are prudish, aren't you? I was told that you were, but I didn't believe it.'

'Now you've found out for yourself. Goodnight, Roddy.'

Sarah slid swiftly out of the car and hurried towards the front door, fumbling in her bag for her latch-key.

She was half way upstairs when she heard the sound of the engine, and the car taking off with a rush which would doubtlessly irritate her father when he noticed the tyre tracks in the gravel and pebbles scattered on the grass.

Am I really a prude? she wondered when, having undressed, she stood by the handbasin in her bedroom, taking off her make-up before she brushed her teeth.

The mirror reflected her deep golden leonine eyes, fringed by curling black lashes, said to be a throwback to the impetuous girl from Martinique who had been disowned by her family, wealthy Creoles of French origin, after running away with the penniless, ineligible young man who had been Sarah's great-grandfather.

She had not been a prude, that was certain, but a strong-willed and reckless girl who, for love, had given up everything in an age when it had been much harder for women to follow their hearts.

How she must have adored him, Sarah thought enviously. She found herself aching with longing to be held in the arms of a man whose embraces could never offend her, and whose kisses would fire her own blood.

The next day was her Saturday off. Over a late weekend breakfast, she told her mother and father that Roddy had asked her to marry him, that she could never say yes, and that they had parted with cross words.

By the evening, her mother had begun to accept that her hope of a marriage had been ill-judged. 'Although it does seem a pity,' was her final, disappointed comment.

The morning mail did not come until after Sarah had left for work. On Monday, all morning she felt convinced that the postman had delivered a letter, type-addressed to Miss Sarah Graham, containing a brief, formal note regretting that the vacancy had been filled.

At lunch-time, unable to contain her curiosity until the evening, she rang up her home.

'No, there was nothing for you, dear. Were you expecting something important?' was her mother's reply to her enquiry.

Sarah improvised an excuse about a catalogue she had ordered. As she thought Lyle Talbot a man who would not take long to make a choice, she could only assume that his secretary did not work on Saturday mornings.

She had not been marked down for a night job, but she left the office rather late and did not reach home until shortly before the hour at which her parents dined.

Having entered the house she would have gone directly upstairs to change her clothes before dinner, but her father came out of the sitting-room to intercept her.

'You have a visitor, Sarah.'

'Not Roddy?' she said, in dismay.

Her mother had forecast that, if he had been unpleasant, Roddy would call to apologise. But there had been no car in the drive.

'No, not Roddy,' answered Mr Graham.

He disappeared into the room, and uncertainly Sarah followed him.

'Good evening, Miss Graham,' said Lyle Talbot, rising from the sofa beside her mother to his impressive full height.

CHAPTER TWO

'W-what are you doing here?' Sarah ejaculated.

'I've been here for two hours,' he said calmly. 'Seeing that I'm not to be dislodged, your parents have very kindly invited me to dinner.'

'Actually Mr Talbot came to invite you to have dinner with him, Sarah,' explained her mother. 'Why didn't you tell us you'd met him on Friday evening?'

'Perhaps she forgot that she had,' said Lyle Talbot, looking amused. 'One can forget meeting people.'

'A dull person, yes—but not you,' said Mrs Graham rather archly.

'Perhaps Sarah didn't tell us because Mr Talbot had already offered her a job on his newspaper, and she felt we should want her to turn it down,' suggested her father.

'No, I didn't offer her a job on Friday. I would never do so to someone I'd only just met. But the paper and the island were mentioned,' said the younger man smoothly. 'And that's why I'm here at the moment. If you'd like to visit the West Indies, and join my staff for a year or so, I'd be glad to have you, Miss Graham.'

Sarah stood stunned and speechless—doubly stunned when her mother enthused, 'I think you should accept, darling. It's a wonderful opportunity for you. Mr Talbot has told us all about his plans for the paper and, although I should have reservations about your going off on your own to a place where you didn't know anyone, I feel that we do know him, and you'll be quite safe under his aegis.'

'Your husband may not share your flattering confidence in my probity, Mrs Graham.'

'I'm sure he does, Mr Talbot.'

'Would you be happy for your daughter to come to Compostela, sir?'

'Not happy—no. We should miss her. But I have no objection,' said Mr Graham. 'And as far as her well-being is concerned, Sarah is over twenty-one, and a sensible, level-headed girl who has never caused us any anxiety. She can take care of herself.'

Lyle looked at the still silent Sarah. 'Your parents approve. What do you have to say on the subject, Miss Graham? I can't give you much time to make up your mind, I'm afraid. It has to be yes or no immediately—or at least before I leave here tonight.'

'I think poor Sarah is flabbergasted. Run up to your room and change, dear, and I must attend to our meal,' said Mrs Graham, shepherding her daughter from the room.

In the hall she said, in an undertone, 'He's charming. Has he a wife?'

'I don't know. I shouldn't think so.'

'Why not put on the cashmere sweater you had for Christmas. It suits you, that pale jade colour.'

Sarah gave a low groan. 'Oh, *Mother*! Don't . . . *please* don't start thinking on those lines. It's not on, truly it isn't.'

'I don't know what you mean,' said Mrs Graham. 'I was only suggesting that you put on a pretty sweater which you haven't yet worn.'

She bustled away to her kitchen, and Sarah walked slowly upstairs, unable as yet to take in that the job was hers—if she wanted it.

But did she? That was the question. For this was no straightforward opportunity to see a part of the world which had always held a fascination for her.

It was complicated by the fact that she would be working for a man who had for a long time bewitched her in much the same way. The reality of Compostela might be nothing like her mental picture of it, and already she had reason to

know that the real Lyle Talbot was not without flaw, like
her starry-eyed teenage dream of him.

She changed, but not into the expensive jade cashmere.
She put on the pink velours track suit which she usually
wore at home in the evening. Then she went downstairs to
the kitchen to help her mother, but was firmly shooed back
to the sitting-room where her father and Lyle were talking
Caribbean politics.

Her father had poured out some sherry for her, and she
sat down and sipped it and watched them.

Mr Graham had changed from a suit into a pair of tweed
pants and a sweater over a checked shirt. His guest was
equally informal except that instead of a sweater he was
wearing a lightweight blouson of very soft chamois leather
over an open-necked shirt with a silk scarf inside the collar.

The pale buttermilk colour of the leather emphasised the
darkness of his colouring, and the casual style of the garment underlined the athleticism of his body. He had spoken
of sailing as his relaxation. Sarah's acquaintance with boats
was confined to two Channel crossings on the way to and
from a weekend in Paris with her parents to celebrate her
twentieth birthday, and being taken for a row on the
Serpentine by a boy she had known a short time.

She found herself thinking of Lyle at the helm of a sailing
boat skimming over a clear turquoise sea, and herself sitting
wherever a passenger did sit, en route to a picnic *à deux* on
some deserted coral strand.

I'm becoming as bad as Mother who sees every person-
able man as a prospective husband, she told herself
vexedly. Except that I don't visualise him as a husband,
only as a lover.

She could see very clearly that, if she went to the island,
she would be committing herself to her first real love affair.
If he wanted her, there would be no way she could resist
him.

Why, indeed, should she resist him? As her father had

said a little earlier, she was over twenty-one and independent. Her parents would not approve, but what they didn't know could not hurt them. And anyway, every generation had a different scale of moral values. That Liz had already had two lovers would shock Mrs Graham, if she knew. It hadn't changed Liz from the girl she had been at eighteen into a promiscuous person. She was just the same, only wiser, with deeper insights.

'Supper is ready,' announced Mrs Graham, from the doorway. She led the way into the dining-room. 'Would you sit over there, Mr Talbot.'

He did not go at once to the chair she indicated, but paused to pull out Sarah's chair for her before walking round to his own place.

'I'd prefer it if you all called me Lyle. If your daughter decides to join my staff I shall call her Sarah. I'm sure I can assert my authority, when necessary, without resorting to formality,' he added, with a smile in his eyes as he glanced across the table at Sarah.

'Very well, Lyle it shall be. I must say it's quite impossible to think of you as someone we have only just met,' said her mother. 'I suppose most people who have watched you for years feel they know you.'

'Yes, it can be trying at times. Total strangers feel free to accost me and tell me home-truths, or the long and tedious story of their life,' he answered. 'Having a face known to millions is not an advantage, I assure you. I shall be glad to withdraw into the anonymity of editing.'

'But it must also have some advantages. Good tables in restaurants, and so on.'

'If such things are important—yes. To me, they are not, or not any more. Fortunately, unlike Cromwell, I'm not "damned to everlasting fame". Television performers are very quickly forgotten when they cease to perform regularly.'

'Is your wife in television, too?'

Inwardly, Sarah cringed. She felt sure he was no more deceived by the guilelessness of her mother's question than she was.

'I am not married, Mrs Graham. Up to now my life has been too footloose to make marriage a practicable proposition. And roving news correspondents are not high on the list of insurance companies' good risks, so there would have been little compensation for my widow had I been one of the several unlucky ones who have been killed on the job in recent years.'

He paused, and a sardonic gleam came into his shrewd dark eyes. 'Perhaps that changes your mind about encouraging Sarah to come and work in Compostela. No doubt you would feel a good deal happier if my aegis was shared by my wife.'

Mrs Graham, unaware that she had been recognised as a matchmaking mother, and was being subtly mocked, said brightly, 'Perhaps, without family commitments, you will have more time to help your staff settle in than you might have done otherwise. Have they all been recruited in London?'

'No, if Sarah joins us, only she and I will be coming from Britain. The others will all be West Indies born and bred. My chief reporter is a Barbadian journalist, and the junior is coming from Trinidad. On the works side I have two local men who know how to operate the extremely antiquated equipment for composing and printing the paper. We're going to start as a weekly and hope to become a biweekly. In its heyday, the *Star* in Antigua could sell three issues a week. But conditions have changed a great deal since 1936 when the *Star* was founded. I must be frank with you and warn you that, this time next year, Sarah and I could be back in London, looking for work.'

'Oh, well, that isn't something to worry about,' was her mother's comfortable answer.

'Not for Sarah perhaps, but for me it could be,' said Lyle

dryly. 'However, I shouldn't have embarked on this enterprise if I were not reasonably confident of pulling it off.'

Mrs Graham was an excellent cook whose principal interests in life were to make her husband and daughter as
comfortable as possible, and to feed them with delicious but
well-balanced meals.

Lyle was not flattering her when, having eaten a second
helping of her raspberry shortcake, he complimented her
on her cooking.

The two men returned to the sitting-room while Mrs
Graham made the coffee and Sarah cleared the table and
loaded the dish-washer.

She had taken almost no part in the conversation during
dinner, and now her mind was made up. Not only was she
going to accept the job but if, subsequently, Lyle made a
pass at her, she would go along with that as well. If, in a
year's time, the paper folded or he did not renew her
contract, she would come back to England having broad-
ened her horizons in every sense. If living life to the full
meant risking heartache—so be it.

It was time to put girlhood behind her, and become a
woman. Marie-Martine, her great-grandmother, had
scorned caution and the conventions. No one was going to
shun Sarah for doing what many of her contemporaries did
as a matter of course.

As soon as she announced her decision, the talk turned to
practical matters—the length of notice she must give to her
present editor, the arrangements for her journey to
Compostela, which would be by jumbo jet to Antigua and
thence by a smaller aircraft to the neighbouring island.

When the time came for Lyle to leave, Sarah said she
would drive him to the station.

'There's no need for that. It's only a short walk from
here.'

'There are still some things I want to ask you. I'll go and
bring the car round.'

She went to slip on a jacket and go through the kitchen to the garage where her mother's car was parked alongside her father's.

The door was an up-and-over, operated by a switch from inside and by an electronic beam from outside. As she backed the car out of the garage and steered it towards the front door, she saw him and her parents in the porch. He towered above them, a light-coloured mac folded and laid over his shoulder as he shook hands and bade them goodnight.

She leaned over to open the passenger door, and a few moments later he was folding himself into the seat beside her and pulling the door shut.

She had never realised before what an intimate place a car was when shared with a man who could just about keep his long legs from impeding her use of the gear lever, but who, to accommodate his shoulders, had to sit half-turned with his right upper arm along the back of her seat, and his forearm raised to the roof.

'I should have brought Father's car. You're too large for a Mini,' she said lightly.

'Too large for many things,' he answered. 'In places where people are on the short side, such as Spain and South America, if I want to sleep comfortably I have to take a double room and lie diagonally. Otherwise my feet hang over the end of the bed.'

'I suppose so.'

Why, when he said the word bed, did it instantly conjure up a vision of a moonlit bedroom in the tropics, and Lyle making love to her? Just that one word, spoken by him, and it had a far greater effect than all Roddy's passionate kisses.

'What was it you wanted to ask me?' he said, as they drove out of the gates.

'Why did you come here in person, instead of writing or telephoning?'

'It seemed a reasonable courtesy to present myself to

your parents before taking their only daughter a long way from home,' was his answer. 'It was immediately obvious that you hadn't mentioned the job to them, so without actually telling a lie, I implied that you and I had met through the girl friend with whom you had supper after seeing me. Then I told them about my paper, and how I'd heard about you from Bob and Maggie and wanted to offer you a job. Wasn't that the best way to handle it?'

'Yes, it was—very tactful indeed.' She explained her reason for keeping the interview a secret. 'You must be very quick on the uptake.'

'I believe I have that reputation.' He paused. 'I think both our antennae picked up your mother's thought waves when she asked me if I had a wife. You needn't have felt any embarrassment. It's the usual maternal reflex when any man comes within range. She's a fond, domesticated wife who would like to see you fulfilling the same role. Did she have a career before her marriage?'

'My grandfather was a dentist. She was his receptionist for a while. That was how she met Father, when he came to have his teeth checked.'

He said, 'If there was a man in your life, you wouldn't be coming to Compostela. Where does marriage come in your scheme of things?'

'I suppose when I fall in love with someone who loves me. At twenty-one, I'm not in any great hurry. Are you worried that I might break my contract with you?'

'No, although if you did it would be difficult to replace you without a good deal of inconvenience.'

They had arrived at the station. Lyle asked how often the trains ran. Told there would be a ten-minute wait, he wound down the window in his door—it was not a particularly cold night—and seemed disposed to wait in the car, in spite of the limited leg-room.

'When are you returning to Compostela?' Sarah asked.

'It depends. I'm working on the narration for a documentary programme which another man and I have scripted. It's a subject which could sell States-side, and make us both a lot of money. So I may be around for a couple of weeks or a month.'

But he did not suggest they should meet again. Instead, he said, 'I take it you'll tell Bob you're leaving first thing tomorrow?'

'Yes.'

'Naturally the other reporters will want to know where you're going, but I'd rather you didn't mention me. I don't want any publicity to attach to my retirement from television. In any case, apart from Bob, Jack is the only person who was on the *News* in my time. The rest of the staff have joined the paper since I left it.'

'Very well, I won't mention your name.'

'Compostela isn't a malarial area,' he added, 'nor need you worry about typhoid. But it might be as well to have a polio booster. Don't go buying yourself a mass of clothes. You'll find the shops on the island have much more attractive resort clothes than anything on sale in London.'

How did he know that? she wondered. Clearly, a woman had told him, a woman interested in fashion.

'If you have any queries or problems, you can contact my secretary,' was his last remark, before he got out of the car. 'Goodnight, Sarah.' With a casual pat on her shoulder, he withdrew his arm from behind her. Seconds later he was disappearing into the station building.

As she drove the short distance home, Sarah wondered if the real reason he did not want his name mentioned was because he thought it might cause Jack to make some derogatory remarks about him. She was not certain if Jack knew about his wife's pre-marital affair with Lyle.

Rosemary had confided in Sarah one night when she had been supposed to baby-sit for them. At the last moment their toddler had been sick and feverish, and Rosemary had not wanted to leave him. As the function they had been attending had been a working assignment for Jack, he had had to go on his own, leaving Sarah to keep his wife company.

It had been later in the evening, when the child had fallen asleep and the two girls were having a snack supper, that Rosemary had switched on the television, seen Lyle's face on the screen, and instantly switched the set off again.

When Sarah had questioned the action, she had triggered an hour-long confession which had caused her almost as much disillusionment as it had to Rosemary at the time when, at the height of a passionate romance, Lyle had suddenly changed his job and left her flat.

Not unexpectedly, as soon as Sarah re-entered the house her mother began to chatter excitedly about her new job.

'I'm amazed you approve,' said Sarah.

'Well, I can see you're quite adamant about not marrying Roddy, and this way there won't be any awkwardness while he gets over his disappointment. Besides——'

Mrs Graham glanced at her husband, and paused before she continued, 'Besides, I know how much you've always wanted to visit the island where your father was born, and he says, if you're working there, he might think of spending a holiday there.'

'Really, Dad? That would be wonderful,' Sarah exclaimed.

'We'll see,' he said, smiling at her.

She had a shrewd notion that, during her absence, he had had a restraining talk with her mother, and that what Mrs Graham had been going to say, before she remembered his strictures, was that the failure of her previous marriage plan was less disappointing now that an even more eligible parti had appeared on the scene.

It wasn't until the next morning, as they were driving to work together, that she said to her father, 'What did you think of Lyle, Dad? I supposed you must have liked him, or you wouldn't have been in favour of my working for him.'

'I certainly saw nothing to dislike. The main reason I am in favour is that I think all young people need to spread their wings for a year or two. Your mother will miss you even more than I shall—you and I are the keystones of her life—and I don't like to see her unhappy. But nor do I want to see you urged into an unsuitable marriage. You're still very young, and youthful marriages have a higher rate of failure than those contracted by more mature couples.'

She said, 'Dad, I've never asked you—although I've discussed it with Mother—but what do you think about having affairs before marriage? Everyone seems to nowadays, and sometimes I wonder if I'm missing something.'

'That's a very difficult question for a father to answer, Sarah. No man likes to think of his daughter being involved in any relationship less secure and permanent than marriage to a thoroughly estimable young man. However, as a lawyer I have to be a realist, and nowadays when the risk of unwanted children is greatly reduced—by no means eliminated, unfortunately—I have to admit that if two young people are overpoweringly attracted to each other, but have little else in common, it's probably better for them to work off the attraction in the course of a temporary liaison rather than to marry and divorce.'

Mr Graham paused to slow the car to allow a motorist to enter the rush-hour stream from a side-street.

'But, having said that,' he went on, 'I believe the majority of affairs and trial marriages show a want of stability and maturity in one or both partners. There are not many marriages which won't work if both parties try their best. Selfishness is the rock on which most marriages founder.'

The traffic was moving so slowly that he could take one hand from the wheel to give her arm an affectionate squeeze.

'I don't think you need feel you've missed out, my dear. But I hope you know that whatever you choose to do in life, your mother and I will always be ready to give you any help you need, and will love you as much as we always have.'

'Thank you, Dad. I do know that,' she said huskily.

At work, at the first opportunity, she told Bob she wanted to leave.

He did not seem greatly surprised. 'I wondered if you'd seen that advertisement. I shall be sorry to lose you, but I didn't really expect to keep you much longer, Sarah. It's the nature of most young reporters to have itchy feet. Fleet Street used to be their mecca, until industrial disputes put half the nationals out of business, and television introduced a new form of journalism. I remember Lyle's youthful ambitions. He was going to the top—and he got there. But being a sound man at bottom, he's since discovered that success is often a snare and a delusion. There used to be a song which put it in a nutshell. Can't remember the tune, but part of the lyric was—*Fame, if you win it, comes and goes in a minute*. Very true, that, especially in television.'

'Yes, I know that song. It goes on—*What is the best thing to cling to? Someone to love you, just one someone to love you* . . . But I gather Lyle hasn't settled for that yet. In fact I've heard on the grapevine that he is, or has been, a womaniser,' Sarah said casually.

Bob took off and polished his spectacles. He was seated behind his big desk with its battery of spikes and trays holding copy waiting to be subbed, copy ready to be set, and the rough proofs called pulls.

Sarah was by the window, two storeys above the busy shopping street where the *News* building was sandwiched between a dry cleaners and a greengrocers specialising in West Indian vegetables—ackee, breadfruit, taro, cassava, christophene, mangoes and pigeon peas.

If she had looked down at the people passing along the pavements, the majority would have been dark-skinned. This was an area of the capital which had become home from home for the older ones among them, and was the only home they had known for the younger ones. They might have the physical characteristics of people from far-away lands, but their accents were purest Cockney.

A youth with a Chinese face would call out, 'Wotcher, Curly.' And a lad who could have been an African would shout back, 'Wotcher, mate.' They had known each other since primary school and were both born-and-bred young Londoners, growing up in a racial melting-pot from which Bob hoped there would spring a peaceful, well-ordered community which no longer provided incidents for certain papers to sensationalise.

'Yes, I think he was at one time,' he replied to Sarah's remark. 'What he's like now, I wouldn't know. But I think I can safely say that he won't bother you in that way if you don't give him any encouragement. He's no seducer of young girls.'

'I'm not exactly a dewy-eyed seventeen-year-old!'

'Are there any left?' he said acidly. Then he laughed. 'Yes, I daresay there are. One doesn't hear about them. It's the hardboiled minxes of that age who attract attention.' He replaced his spectacles. 'Anyway, I wish you well, Sarah—and I certainly envy you the climate. Now I'd better get busy and advertise for a replacement for you.'

That evening she left the office to find Roddy waiting for her.

'Sarah, I'm sorry. Forgive me for being such a boor,' were his opening words, as he stepped in her path.

'Of course. It was my fault, too. Let's forget it ever happened, shall we?'

'May I run you home?' he asked. 'I had to park the car round the corner.'

'Thank you, but I'm not going home yet. I'm working this evening.'

'Then let me take you wherever you're going.'

'The meeting doesn't start until half past seven. At the moment I'm on my way to the Public Library to do some more research on the island where I'm going to work. I didn't know it the other night, but I've been accepted for a job on the *Compostela Independent*.'

He looked shattered. 'Where's Compostela?'

'Oh, Roddy, your geography's terrible! It's one of the Leeward Islands. Surely you must have heard of Antigua, Anguilla and St. Kitts, even if not of all of them.'

'I thought Compostela was in Spain.'

'You're thinking of Santiago de Compostela where the mediaeval pilgrims used to go. *My* Compostela was named after it when Columbus discovered the island in 1493, in the same way that Antigua was named after a Madonna in Seville, Santa Maria la Antigua.'

'But why go and work on an island in the back of beyond? You must be crazy!' Roddy expostulated.

'It's where my father was born, and his father before him. It's where my roots are.'

'Oh, for God's sake, Sarah, that's nonsense. You belong here—with me,' he added, seizing her hands. 'Look, we can't talk here in the street. What a crummy neighbourhood this is'—with a glance of distaste as two very stout West Indian women waddled past, chatting cheerfully together.

'You're such a snob, Roddy,' Sarah said mildly. 'Everyone can't live in large houses with tennis courts and three-car garages.'

He ignored this. 'Is there a decent café near here?'

Realising that there was no way to avoid a tête-à-tête, she took him to a fairly quiet tea-shop where, for nearly an hour, he argued and protested, abasing himself in the hope of winning her round.

Sarah didn't want him to plead. As she listened, she couldn't help thinking that Lyle would never beg to be loved. He would either make a woman love him, or, if he couldn't, say nothing of his own feelings. He would scorn to offer as inducements the material things Roddy was dangling. Her own car. Accounts at the best shops.

'I'm sorry, Roddy. I'm just not ready to marry yet,' she told him, feeling that this was less hurtful than saying bluntly, *I don't love you.* 'I'm tremendously excited about this job, and nothing would induce me to give up the chance to visit such a lovely part of the world.'

It was an upsetting encounter from which she was glad to escape to the meeting she had to cover.

The next day her contract arrived; an agreement to work for Lyle for twelve months. Sarah signed it, and sent it back. She heard nothing more from him until, one night a week later, he telephoned while she was out. He left a message with her father.

'Lyle has arranged for you to fly out together,' he told her. 'You'll be stopping overnight in Antigua, and finishing the journey the next morning. He'll take care of all the arrangements. We shall see you off at the airport, and then you'll have him to look after you until you arrive at the house where you will be living.'

'It's the home of a Methodist minister,' went on her mother. 'So you couldn't be in better hands. It's very thoughtful of Lyle to arrange such impeccable lodgings. A young girl on her own in a new place can't be too careful.'

Sarah had spent the afternoon shopping in the West End. Although winter cruise wear was available, she had taken Lyle's advice not to buy any clothes. But, half-guiltily, she had equipped herself with a mini-trousseau of pretty underclothes and one exquisite and very expensive nightdress, in case he invited her to share an unofficial honeymoon with him.

To find that she was to be housed with a clergyman and his family was disconcerting. But perhaps it was only a temporary arrangement.

Bob had said that Lyle was not a seducer of young girls.

But twenty-one was grown-up by anyone's standards, and seduction implied the coercion of a girl's will. She would not be unwilling; she was eager to learn about love from him.

Even her father had conceded that sometimes there were overwhelming attractions which were better worked out of the system, leaving the mind and heart clear for a more durable relationship.

Now Lyle was no longer a daydream. Fate, or chance, had thrown them together, and the time had arrived for her to stop holding back, to start Living with a capital L.

If, with a little encouragement, Lyle would teach her some of his expertise, then encouragement was what she would give him.

CHAPTER THREE

THE right clothes for a journey from the middle of an English winter to the perpetual summer of the Caribbean required careful thought. Finally Sarah decided that, as she would be travelling to Heathrow Airport in her father's car, she would wear a lightweight carnation red suit bought the previous spring. The material didn't crease easily, and the skirt had a flare which would be more comfortable than a straight line on a flight lasting eight hours. Under the jacket she would wear a red silk shirt, with a short-sleeved pink shirt in her hand luggage to change into just before landing.

Although she did wear other colours, dark red and deep pink were her favourites. With her colouring, the neutrals didn't suit her, except camel which emphasised her tawny eyes.

To her surprise, since the cost of her fare was included in their agreement, Lyle had chosen to fly first class. His secretary, with whom she had had several telephone conversations, had explained that he always flew first on a long flight, finding the seating in the other classes too confined for a man of his size.

Because of this Sarah had a baggage allowance which allowed her to pack a selection of well-loved books, her cassette player and some tapes, and various things from her bedroom which would help to make her feel at home in her digs.

The night before leaving England was a restless one for her. Having flown before, she wasn't nervous on that score, but the thought of eight hours in the closest proximity to Lyle made her inside churn with mingled excitement and apprehension.

Very early on her last morning at home, she slipped out of bed for a final check through her belongings.

Her hand luggage consisted of her bag, containing passport, tickets, travellers' cheques, her driving licence and address book; her portable Japanese typewriter, and the airline cabin bag issued free to first class passengers. In this she had a pair of flat mules to wear in the air, her pink shirt, a couple of paperbacks and, in separate zip packs, her make-up and toilet articles.

Her two matching suitcases, the smaller one soft-topped, were already locked, strapped and labelled, with additional labels inside them in case they should go astray.

Although the house at Kew was not the only home she had ever known, they had moved there when she was six, and her memories of their previous house were blurred. As she looked at the familiar surroundings in which, except when on holiday, she had woken up every morning for the past fifteen years, she found it hard to grasp that tomorrow she would be dressing not only far from home, but far from her parents as well.

At breakfast her mother was inclined to be tearful. Sarah and her father strove to be cheerful, but their conversation was forced.

It was not a long way from their home to the airport, but they set out in plenty of time in case of unforeseen delays. Lyle had arranged, through his secretary, to meet them in the public concourse of the terminal for international flights.

He was not there when they arrived, and this agitated Mrs Graham, a person who preferred to hang about for half an hour beforehand rather than risk being one second late for an appointment.

Lyle had a different attitude to punctuality. He arrived two or three minutes in advance of the time arranged, his calm manner that of someone long accustomed to world-wide travels.

He shook hands with them, making a comment about the morning's news to her father, affecting not to notice her mother's brimming eyes, but taking in the details of Sarah's appearance as he clasped her hand.

'I'm sorry I haven't been able to talk to you myself since our last meeting, Sarah,' he said. 'But I've been exceedingly busy, and Joan is an efficient go-between. You haven't checked in yet, I see'—glancing at her cases. 'Shall we do that now?'

His own luggage consisted of one large case of the kind in which suits and shirts could be packed on hangers and emerge with minimal creasing. Like her, he had a typewriter with him.

When their cases had been weighed, tagged and whisked away on a conveyor belt, not to be seen again until Antigua, he said to her father, 'Long-drawn-out farewells are more painful than brisk ones, Mr Graham. I think Sarah and I should go through to the passenger lounge now. Goodbye, sir. Goodbye, Mrs Graham.'

With an inclination of his head, he walked away, leaving them to take leave of their daughter without an onlooker.

Saying goodbye was painful for them all. Her mother broke down and cried. Her father's face took on the set look of a British-bred male trying to batten down deep emotion. Sarah's own throat was tight.

They embraced, murmured half incoherent farewells, and then Mr Graham led his weeping wife towards the exit, and Sarah turned in the direction taken by Lyle, her own tears unshed but making everything shimmer.

While they had their tickets and passports inspected, she found it hard to control her distress at seeing her mother in tears.

As soon as they entered the passenger lounge, Lyle said,

'You can leave your typewriter and cabin bag with me. The women's room is over there if you want to retire for five minutes. We have plenty of time. There's no hurry.'

She emerged from the washroom composed, and saw him at a table near the bar, drinking coffee, with another cup waiting for her.

He rose when he saw her approaching.

'You must think us very sentimental,' she said awkwardly, when she joined him.

'Not at all. A close-knit, affectionate family is something to be envied nowadays. Have you brought any reading material? If not, there's a good selection of paperbacks over there'—indicating a shopping area.

Presently it was announced on the tannoy that their flight was boarding at Gate 23, and they began the long walk to the waiting aircraft. Lyle carried her typewriter for her, and matched his long stride to hers.

A group of cleaners coming in the opposite direction recognised him, and nudged each other. One of them said, 'Good morning, Mr Talbot,' and he grinned and answered, 'Good morning, ladies.' Their giggles, and a whispered, 'Who's she?', followed them along the walkway.

She found that the first class passengers were accommodated in a section in the nose of the aircraft, with a spiral staircase at the rear leading up to a double-decker area which included the flight deck.

Between her window seat and Lyle's was a drinks-rest on which, very soon after take-off, there were two glasses of champagne.

It wasn't long before the aircraft had risen above the thick layer of cloud into the bright upper air. The sun, the champagne, her companion, and the extra comforts of first class travel all conspired to lift Sarah's spirits. The sadness of parting from her much-loved parents was replaced by a feeling of excitement at beginning a journey across the

Atlantic with a man who made her intensely aware of being feminine.

'You're wearing a different scent today,' he said suddenly. 'A farewell present from a disconsolate boy-friend?'

She left the question unanswered. 'How do you know it's a different one?'

'It isn't what you were wearing the night you drove me to the station. That, I believe, was Diorissimo, or at any rate lilies of the valley. What's this one?'

'It's by Yves St Laurent—Opium.'

Lyle tilted a quizzical eyebrow. 'Someone sees you as a *femme fatale*, I gather?'

Sarah's cheeks warmed. She wasn't going to admit that she had bought it for herself in her bid for a more sophisticated image.

'You must have a very acute sense of smell.'

'Being a non-smoker helps. I only recognise a few. Arpège, which my mother always wore, and Femme which is my sister's favourite.'

Sarah thought, and Diorissimo which, presumably, was the favourite of one of your more memorable girl-friends.

Aloud, she asked, 'Where does your sister live?'

'For the time being in Washington D.C. She's married to a political correspondent. She used to be a fashion model. You've probably seen her in *Vogue*. She's one inch under six foot, a source of great gloom when she was in her teens. Then a photographer spotted her potential and made her famous and successful, but not particularly happy. That came when she met my brother-in-law whom she says she would have married even if she'd had to look down at him. But he's around my height.'

'Has she given up modelling?' asked Sarah.

'Yes, she's busy having babies. You'll probably meet her before long. She wants to see the house I've leased. The Government of Compostela has a scheme to prevent the island's old plantation houses from falling into ruins or losing their character. They lease them at peppercorn rents to tenants who will undertake to keep them in good repair. My place is called Emerald Hill.'

'What a lovely name—but how big is the house? A plantation house sounds like a mansion.'

'A small mansion—yes. But I shan't be a bachelor for ever. Raine—my sister—tells me it's time I was thinking of marriage.'

'And are you?' she asked him lightly.

'Not immediately, although Emerald Hill could certainly do with a woman's touch. But I daresay I shall be able to enlist some feminine assistance without going to any extreme lengths, or not until the paper is on its feet,' was his casual reply.

Soon afterwards luncheon was served, a much better meal than Sarah had eaten on any of her previous flights.

Afterwards she watched the movie, and Lyle made up some of the sleep he said he had lost the night before—although for what reason was something he left unexplained. It could have been work which had kept him awake into the small hours, or it could have been an ardent farewell.

Although the film held Sarah's attention most of the time, there were moments when she could not help glancing at the man beside her.

In repose his features suggested a curious mixture of sternness and sensuality. Perhaps the overriding impression was one of authority; authority over himself, and the power to command other people.

She had seen the former in action one night on television when he had been reporting an insurrection and, suddenly, the battle for the city had erupted close to the spot on which he and the cameraman had chosen to film the report. Shells had started to land so close that the camera had shuddered with the impact. Lyle's dark face had glistened with sweat, and each explosion had made him flinch. It had been obvious to the viewers that both men were in imminent danger of being obliterated. But they had held their ground until the report was finished, and if it had been folly on their part not to run for cover—if indeed there had been any cover in that ravaged area—it had also been an act of great courage.

Suddenly, after her gaze had lingered on his sleeping face for longer than she had intended, she became aware of a woman on the other side of the gangway watching her with a slight smile.

Sarah returned her attention to the screen, and kept it there for the rest of the film.

Lyle slept until the cabin staff started to serve afternoon tea, by which time the cloud had dispersed apart from some cotton-wool cumulus floating in the infinity of space between them and the cornflower-blue ocean.

He went to wash and, as he returned, Sarah went to change her shirt.

'Did you enjoy the film?' he asked, as they resumed their seats.

'Yes, it was excellent, thank you. How was your nap?'

'Refreshing. My system is now so accustomed to changing time-zones and sleeping whenever it's convenient that I rarely suffer from jet-lag. But you'll find you will for a few days. By eight o'clock this evening, local time, you'll be longing for bed, but at three in the morning you're likely to be wide awake again.'

Having made the journey before, he knew when she would be able to catch her first glimpse of the island where they were to spend the night.

'There's Antigua,' he said, leaning close to her to point out the land now in view. From her father's description of Compostela, she had expected the islands to be patches of green. But seen from the air Antigua was brown and barren-looking.

She was conscious, not of the thrill of seeing her first Caribbean island, but of a different kind of excitement because he was looking over her shoulder, and she could feel his breath on her ear as he said, 'It's been a dry year, and anyway Antigua only has one small area of rain forest vegetation. What you're seeing from here is a "cassie" area, where nothing much grows but grass and acacia bushes. Compostela is like Montserrat, more mountainous and much more lush.'

The Grahams always took their holidays in the spring or the autumn, avoiding the crowds of the high season months in Europe. Only in England's rare heatwaves had Sarah experienced before the heat which blazed down on them when, after the aircraft had landed, they descended the steps to the tarmac.

It was even hotter inside the airport, and the plastic upholstery in the taxi would have been uncomfortable had it not been protected from the sun by very gay cotton covers made from hundreds of snippets of fabric, something in the style of a rag rug.

It was not a long drive from the airport to their hotel where, after they had registered, she was led in one direction and Lyle in another.

Before they separated, he said, 'The first thing we'll do is to cool off in the sea. I'll come to your room in ten minutes.'

The curtains were drawn in her room, but when the baggage porter pulled a cord they swept apart to reveal a view of green lawns, shaded by palm trees, sweeping down to a wide stretch of sand lapped by water the colour of aquamarines.

Mindful that it wouldn't be long before Lyle reappeared, Sarah unlocked the case containing her two bikinis.

One had lime green leaves on a white ground, the other was made of stretchy apricot velours with gilt links on the hips and where the neck ties joined the scanty triangles of the top part.

She put it on, hung up her travelling clothes, put one or two things in a beach bag, and continued unpacking until she heard Lyle's knock.

She went to open the door.

'Ready?' he asked.

Swiftly his dark eyes appraised her, noting her small firm breasts, slender waist and the curves of her hips. The quick but comprehensive scrutiny might have unnerved her had she not been unable to prevent herself from taking in the splendours of his physique.

With his clothes on, Lyle's breadth of shoulders and lithe, upright bearing suggested a lot of muscle and little if any spare flesh. Undressed, he was an impressive example of what a human being could look like if he didn't abuse his body with over-eating and lack of exercise. Not that many men had his proportions; the wide shoulders matched by the long, strong column of his neck and by legs which were sinewy but slim.

There was nothing of the gorilla about him, as there was about some large, powerful men. He reminded her more of the big cats, the tiger and the panther with their soft-stepping elegance of movement, and the sleek outlines which only bunched with muscle when they sprang.

He was wearing a beach garment which was new to her; a kind of short sarong of towelling which covered him from hip to mid-thigh and evidently doubled as a towel as he wasn't carrying a separate one. It was khaki-coloured, bound with black, with a pocket for the few things a man took to the beach.

She said, 'I'll just get my bag and towel.'

Having done so, she locked her door and walked with him along the verandah beneath the bougainvillea-garlanded balcony leading to the bedrooms above those which, like hers, were on the ground floor.

'Is your room satisfactory?' he asked.

'Very, thank you—and what a glorious outlook!'

'Yes, I think this is a pleasant hotel, as indeed the majority are here. So far the Antiguans have been sensible and avoided the high-rise building which has ruined too many beautiful places.'

As they turned the corner at the end of the terrace and began to cross the garden towards the beach, he said, 'To observe the proprieties as far as possible, I made a point of asking for our rooms to be in different blocks. But there are bound to be people who, seeing us together here, will draw the wrong conclusion. Does that bother you?'

Suspecting him of teasing her, she said, 'Not in the least.'

It was true. She would have disliked that assumption about herself and any other man, but not with Lyle.

'Lots of girls have to travel with their employers,' she added airily.

'True. Some of the attractive girls seen here with older men are airline stewardesses on a rest stop with the male crew.'

They saw a couple of unused sun beds in the partial shadow of a palm and walked towards them. People whose skin-colour ranged from winter-white with lobster patches to the deep gold result of at least ten days' careful tanning lay about in the sun or the shade, or stood chatting waist-deep in water, or perched on tall stools round the beach bar with its overhanging thatched roof.

As Lyle and Sarah strolled by, most people looked at them with the interest of established hotel guests inspecting the latest arrivals. Some smiled and said hello.

By the sun beds, Lyle ripped open the Velcro fastening of his updated loincloth. Underneath it were very brief black stretch briefs. His skin was the colour of old bronze, much darker than anyone else's except for a group of Antiguan children romping in the shallows some distance away.

They, and many of the local people Sarah had noticed while at the airport, looked as if, were they to return to the

Guinea coast homes of their forebears, physically if not culturally they would be indistinguishable from the Africans still living there. But even an hour on the island was enough to show that many other Antiguans were the product of two or more racial strains.

Side by side they walked into the sea, but as soon as they began to swim Lyle outdistanced her in a few strokes.

Sarah changed from a crawl to a breast stroke in order to watch him pull ahead. It gave her a foolish glow of pride to see him surging through the sea with his black head half under the surface, and his arms glistening in the sunlight as they rose and fell with the deceptively leisurely movements of the powerful swimmer.

She chided herself for her absurdity. He was not hers to take a pride in. He didn't belong to any woman, and perhaps never would, even though he had spoken as if marriage were a possibility if the *Compostela Independent* was successful and if he decided to settle on the island permanently.

She stopped both swimming and watching him, and lay back, her arms wide, floating. Above her some fluffy white clouds, like those she had noticed from the aeroplane, were drifting across the blue sky, driven by the trade winds blowing into the Caribbean Sea from the vast Atlantic and cooling the islands as they passed.

'This is better than the rush hour in London, or any other big city, wouldn't you say?'

Lyle had come back and was treading water a few feet away from her.

'It's idyllic,' Sarah agreed. 'But how many islanders enjoy this? Aren't these beaches mainly for tourists?'

He shook his head. 'There are no reserved beaches here or in Compostela, and before and after working hours, and on Sundays and public holidays you'll see a lot of the local people sharing the beaches with the visitors. Not the older generations so much, although sometimes a massive old dear will come down and paddle while keeping an eye on her grandchildren.'

They stayed in the warm, clear water for about half an hour until he said, 'Time to try your first rum punch.'

Before taking her to the beach bar, he wrapped the piece of khaki towelling round his lean hips, removed his briefs from beneath it, squeezed them hard in one fist and thrust them into his pocket.

'Will you be uncomfortable in that?' he asked, looking at Sarah's wet bikini. 'Do you want to go back to your room and change before we have a drink?'

She shook her head. 'In this heat, it will be dry in ten minutes.'

She perched on one of the stools while the bar steward mixed equal amounts of lime, orange and pineapple juice with an ounce of red grenadine syrup and two ounces of local light rum. This he poured over several ice cubes and topped with some grated nutmeg before he handed it to her.

Lyle had something called a rum neat which turned out to be a glass of rum and another of iced water. His long legs enabled him to straddle his stool with his feet on the ground, whereas Sarah's rested on the cross-bar.

'Here's to smooth editorial relations,' he said as he lifted the glass with the topaz-coloured spirit in it.

'To smooth relations,' she echoed, mentally including their personal as well as their professional relationship.

Almost as if he read her thought, he said, 'Actually you are not officially my employee until eight o'clock on Monday morning. Our agreement isn't in force yet.'

Why did he remind her of that fact? And watch her with that enigmatic expression?

She veiled her own eyes with her lashes, and raised the straw to her lips to taste the refreshingly cold punch.

'I can't quite believe I'm here. It's been such a rapid transfer from winter to summer, and from my old life to my new one. I'm not used to changes as you are. I've been in rather a rut.'

'I'm accustomed to changes,' he agreed. 'So accustomed I don't know yet that I can adjust to staying put. It could be that I've lived too long out of a suitcase to be able to settle down here. I may find myself getting restless.'

A couple came up to the bar, and the man took the seat next to Lyle. Having given his order, he said, 'Hi! You're new arrivals, I guess. I'm J. K. Lindstrom from Rhode Island, and this is my wife, Charlene.'

Lyle shook hands and introduced himself. 'And this is Sarah Graham,' he added. 'Miss Graham and I are only here for one night. We're en route from London to Compostela, but not to have a holiday there. We're business associates. You're on vacation, I imagine?'

A conversation ensued which lasted until Sarah finished her drink and said, 'I think I'll go and have a shower.'

Lyle said, 'We'll have dinner as soon as the restaurant opens tonight, because you'll be too tired later. I'll meet you in the bar at seven. There's no need to dress up on a week night.'

She nodded, said, 'See you later, I expect,' to Charlene, and smiled at J.K. As she walked away she heard Lyle ordering another drink. By arranging to meet her in the bar, had he been emphasising to the Lindstroms that he and she had no closer association than the one he had mentioned to them earlier?

It was difficult to be sure of his attitude to her. At times he behaved as if she were a very young girl for whom he was in some measure responsible. At other times he seemed to imply that she shouldn't think herself safe with him. She wasn't sure where she stood.

In the shower she shampooed her hair and debated what

to wear for dinner. It was now six o'clock, local time, but in England it would be eleven and her parents would be thinking about going to bed.

As she stepped out of the shower and wrapped herself in a bath sheet, the telephone rang in her bedroom. Thinking it could only be Lyle, she lifted the receiver.

'Hello?'

An unfamiliar voice said, 'Your call to London is through, Miss Graham. Go ahead, please.'

'Sarah? Is that you, dear?' It was her mother speaking now. 'We were wondering if we should call you, but we didn't want you to think we were fussing. But I'm so glad you've called us, darling. How was your flight?'

'Fine, Mother—very enjoyable. I've just been for a swim.'

As she had a brief chat with them both, she realised it must have been Lyle who had booked the call for her. She had thought of telephoning, but had not done so because he was sure to find out when he paid the hotel bill, and might have thought it the act of a girl who was already homesick.

His reactions were of surpassing importance to her; more important even than her parents' feelings. That was how it should be if one loved a man: except that she felt it was foolish to allow it to happen when the love was all on one side.

Before dressing she smoothed herself all over with body lotion, and added a coat of Pink Diamonds varnish to her finger and toenails. Then she put on a pale lemon dress bought the previous summer, and added her butterfly earrings and the golden initial on a chain.

He was not in the bar when she arrived, and she was the first person there. Dinner was served until nine-thirty and probably most people there didn't dine before eight. Rather than sitting by herself, she decided to look in the window of the hotel's boutique. It wasn't open at this hour, but most of the things on display were visible from the plate-glass door.

She was tilting her head to read the price ticket on a pair of shell ear-rings when a woman's voice said, 'Good evening,' and she turned to find a fellow passenger standing beside her. It was the woman who had seen her studying Lyle while he was asleep.

They chatted for a few minutes about the flight and the hotel, and then, at precisely the moment when Lyle himself came within earshot, the woman said, 'I can't think of anywhere lovelier to spend a honeymoon. I hear there are lots of little beaches where one can be completely secluded. Are you and your husband hiring a car while you're here?'

'Mr Talbot isn't my husband,' said Sarah, as he joined them. 'I'm Sarah Graham, Mrs . . .?'

'Burnett. Laura Burnett. How do you do, Mr Talbot?' Obviously she did not recognise him, and later it came out that, although British, she and her husband had never lived in England, having retired to Spain after a lifetime *en poste* in the diplomatic service.

To Sarah she added, 'I'm so sorry, I don't know why I assumed you were on your honeymoon. Perhaps because my husband and I are, in a manner of speaking. We were married during the war—the Second World War—and our honeymoon then consisted of a weekend in an hotel near the base from which he was flying. Now we're celebrating our fortieth anniversary with all the things we missed then, not least some delicious food instead of Woolton pie and dehydrated eggs, and all the other make-shifts of wartime.'

As the three of them strolled to the bar, Sarah could guess why Laura Burnett had assumed they were honeymooners. She must have been gazing at Lyle with her feelings clearly exposed. It mustn't happen again.

'As you aren't on your honeymoon after all, and you're

only here overnight, why not join us for dinner?' Mrs
Burnett suggested presently, after her husband had joined
them.

He, an enthusiastic helmsman, had quickly established a
rapport with Lyle. Thus it was that the dinner *à deux* which
Sarah had expected turned into an innocuous foursome.

By the time they were having coffee, her body was refus-
ing to adjust to not being in bed and asleep at its accustomed time. The Burnetts, by nature night-birds, were
bearing up better than she, and Lyle, having slept on the
plane, was his usual alert self.

'Bedtime for you, I think, Sarah,' he said, seeing her
clench her teeth against the fifth or sixth yawn.

'Would you excuse me? I'm afraid I just can't keep
awake,' she said to Mrs Burnett.

'Of course, my dear. Off you go. Sleep well. We'll see you
at breakfast.'

The two men rose to their feet as she stood up to leave.
Before she was quite out of earshot, she heard Mrs Burnett
remark, 'What a charming girl!'

But she could not catch Lyle's response, and she knew
that what a person in her sixties found charming was not
necessarily what a man in his thirties looked for in the
women in his private life.

She slept until four in the morning, and then lay awake for
an hour until she could bear her inactivity no longer and,
moving quietly, in case the walls should be thin, began to
repack her suitcase.

The glamorous nightdress was in the case she had not
unpacked. In case her mother should catch her in it and
wonder what had possessed her to buy such a garment
when she usually wore Tana lawn nighties, she had never
dared to try it on. Now she took it from its folds of tissue and
slipped it over her head, the diaphanous folds of apricot

chiffon resting as lightly as butterflies' wings on the curves of her slender young body.

All the edges were narrowly bound with apricot satin, and satin ribbons drew the fullness into a high Empire line and tied in a flowing bow at the point of the wide, low-cut V. But it was the transparency of the fabric which made the nightdress seductive. The fineness of the pure silk chiffon made the garment very little more than a cloud of beautiful colour drifting round her breasts, hips and thighs in a way which was anything but virginal.

How long would it be before she wore it for Lyle? she wondered.

CHAPTER FOUR

As soon as it was light she went for a swim. At first the beach was deserted, but she had not been in the water long before she saw Lyle coming to join her.

Near the water's edge he began the sprint for a flying plunge from which he surfaced to ask, 'What time did you wake up?'

'About four. Why are you up so early? I thought you and the Burnetts would probably sit up quite late.'

'We did, but I set my alarm. I like this hour of the day here, just about sunrise. Shall we swim across the bay and then walk back?'

'As long as you don't expect me to keep up with you on the first lap.'

'You could if you had a pair of flippers.' He began to do a lazy back-stroke with which, by exerting herself, Sarah could manage to stay alongside.

It wasn't until they had waded ashore at the other end of the crescent bay that she suddenly remembered the telephone call to her parents. Meeting and having supper with the Burnetts had put it out of her head.

She said, 'I should have thanked you before for arranging the call to London. It was very kind and thoughtful of you.'

'I felt it might reassure your mother to have a few words with her ewe-lamb. She's the one who'll miss you the most.'

Sarah wasn't sure that, at twenty-one, she liked being described as a ewe-lamb, but then she remembered that he had referred to his own mother in the past tense, and asked, 'Are your parents no longer alive?'

66

'They both died some years ago.' His tone held a note of discouragement as if he didn't care for personal questions.

She felt rebuffed. Yet yesterday Lyle had volunteered information about his sister Raine.

By this time the sun had risen, but its warmth was gentle on her skin. The sea gleamed and sparkled in its light. The usual light breeze stirred the graceful fronds of the coconut palms. It was one of life's perfect moments: a memory in the making.

'Is Emerald Hill near the sea?' she asked.

'Yes, it's built on a bluff between two coves. In the past, before electric fans and air-conditioning, houses were always built to take advantage of every breeze, generally on rising ground inland. Now the new breed of settlers—vacationers and retired people—want to live as close to the beach as possible, but it isn't always the best situation.'

All the time they were having breakfast, they were surrounded by the birds she had heard about from her father; dapper black-plumaged greckles, yellow-breasted bananaquits, Zenaida doves and one shimmering dark green hummingbird.

It being lunch-time in England, Sarah was hungry. Instead of her usual light breakfast of fruit juice and bran flakes, she followed Lyle's example and had the hotel's full breakfast.

By nine they were on their way back to the airport for the fifteen-minute flight to Compostela in a Leeward Islands Air Transport plane which seemed tiny by comparison with the transatlantic jumbo of the day before.

The airport was smaller and the formalities briefer at Compostela. When several taxi-drivers converged on him, Lyle shook his head.

'No, thanks—we have our own transport.'

He led Sarah, and the porter carrying their baggage, to a line of cars parked in the shade of some eucalyptus trees. All but one of the cars were unattended. As they approached, the driver opened her door and stepped out.

She was the most spectacularly beautiful girl Sarah had ever laid eyes on, and she was smiling at Lyle as if the sight of him gave her as much pleasure as the sight of her must give him.

'Hello, Vashti. How are you?'

Sarah, a few steps behind, could not see his expression as he took the girl's hand and looked down at her.

'Fine, thank you, Lyle. But very glad to see you back.' Her voice was soft and melodious.

'Vashti, this is Sarah Graham. Vashti is my secretary,' he explained, as he introduced them.

'How do you do, Miss Graham.' The lovely creature held out her hand.

She was simply dressed in a white blouse and black linen skirt, with a black and white belt linking the two. Clearly, many racial strains had combined to produce her extraordinary looks.

Only the women of India had such thick and lustrous black hair, softly waving back from her temples to be caught in a chignon at her nape. Her melting dark eyes had the epicanthus, the little fold at the inner corners of her eyelids which indicated some Chinese genes; and the colour of her flawless complexion was that deep golden brown which results from the mingling of black and white blood, and surpasses any acquired tan, or the paler and darker of human flesh tints.

It would have been impossible for any woman to meet her and not feel diminished by her perfection; and yet, at the same time, to be enthralled by her.

'How do you do, Miss . . .?' Sarah looked enquiringly at Lyle, who had neglected to mention this vision's surname.

'Vashti Safka, but please call me Vashti. May I call you Sarah?' asked the other girl.

'Of course.'

The porter was waiting for the boot of the car to be opened. Vashti moved to unlock it for him. Then she dangled the keys between herself and Lyle.

'Will you drive to town, or shall I?'

'You drive. I'll sit in the back and point things out to Sarah.'

Having tipped the porter, he waited until the two girls were ensconced in the front seats before opening the door of the rear seat.

As they set off, Sarah was conscious that her short curls, though practical for swimming, could not compare for femininity with Vashti's long silky tresses which must reach to her waist when unloosed from their workaday coils. And her chignon, though neater than long hair when she was working, was not unglamorous. In the twisted skeins of blue-black silk she had fixed frangipani flowers, each white petal tipped with deep yellow at the centre.

Next to the charming back view she presented to Lyle, Sarah felt that her own head-hugging crop must look unalluringly boyish.

Many times, during her teen years, she had envied Liz her smooth hair and had thought of having her own straightened. And Liz, born with baby-fine locks without a vestige of curl, had envied her friend's crisp curls and tried perms, never successful.

But not for a very long time had Sarah felt as dissatisfied with her looks as she did as they drove from the airport. She felt Vashti and Lyle were made for each other: two superb human beings as different from ordinary mortals as original Greek statues from the thousands of cheap reproductions made for the tourist market, or a fine pair of Chelsea figures from a mass-produced modern ornament.

What a fool she had been to imagine she would have no competition for Lyle's attentions! But Vashti was unfair competition. No man, least of all Lyle, could have eyes for anyone else while she was around. Her beauty was so exceptional that it was amazing to find her in a small place like Compostela. One would have expected her to have been snapped up by the film world, or for international-class modelling.

Leaning forward to rest his forearms on the back of the bench seat shared by the two girls, Lyle pointed out various landmarks, and Sarah tried to listen attentively.

The television masts and the oil refinery were new since her father's time, but otherwise the island didn't appear to have changed much. Most of the inhabitants still lived in small timber-built houses, painted yellow, soft powder blue and Sarah's favourite bright pink.

The capital was called St James, after the Saint from whose burial place the island took its name. Compostela derived from the Latin *campus stellae*, meaning 'field of the star', a reference to the star which, in the ninth century, had indicated to his disciples where his body, martyred in Palestine, was to be buried.

St James, in her father's time, had been a small, quiet town which only bustled on Saturdays when the country people came in to sell their produce in the wharfside market. Since then the capital had expanded, and the sunlit streets often swarmed with passengers from cruise liners.

'We'll take you straight to your digs, and you can spend the rest of the day doing a little exploring and resting,' said Lyle, as they passed through the centre of the town and headed for the southern suburbs. 'Tomorrow I'm having a lunch party at Emerald Hill where you'll meet your colleagues and others involved in the *Independent*.'

Presently, in a street of well-kept large bungalows with fenced gardens and carports or garages, Vashti stopped the car outside one where a woman was sitting on the porch. She came down the path to meet them; a large-busted Compostelan matron with a few threads of grey in her hair and a friendly smile on her face.

Before Lyle could introduce them, she said warmly, 'I'm Susan Charbonne, my dear. Welcome to our home. We'll do our best to make you comfortable.'

'Thank you . . . how kind,' said Sarah.

It was not unlike being made welcome by her own mother. Mrs. Charbonne was about the same age, and clearly a similar kind of woman, although she and her husband might not be as affluent as the Grahams.

'I'll be showing Miss Graham her room while you bring in her luggage, Mr Talbot. Or maybe I should call you Sarah, as you're the same age as my youngest daughter,' she suggested, as he returned to the car while she led her paying guest inside. 'Mr Talbot has told me all about you,' she added.

The room Sarah was to occupy was spotlessly clean and comfortably furnished, although lacking the co-ordinated décor of her room at home. But if the colour scheme was slightly garish, and the room rather small and without a handbasin, at least it was cheerful and airy. A vase of flowers had been placed on the chest of drawers which, as she discovered a little later, had been lined with fresh paper for her arrival.

'Can I offer you and the other young lady a cup of coffee, Mr Talbot?' Mrs Charbonne enquired, when he rejoined them with the cases.

'No, thank you. We mustn't dawdle, we have a great deal to do,' he answered. 'I'll see you tomorrow at my place, Sarah. Vashti will fetch you about ten. Bring your bikini, and another if you have it—we'll be in and out of the water all day.'

A few moments later he had gone.

Although the Charbonnes had three daughters, none was living at home. The two elder girls were married, and the youngest was working in the Compostela Tourist Office in London. The present household consisted of the Reverend

George Charbonne and his wife, his aged mother, and their teenage son Michael.

That evening, after the five of them had eaten a well-cooked but heavy evening meal, Sarah helped Mrs Charbonne wash up and then retired early to bed.

She closed the door of her room with a sigh of relief at being alone. Like innumerable girls before her, she found settling in rather wearing. The old lady was very deaf, the boy was awkward and tongue-tied in the presence of a stranger. His parents, anxious to be hospitable, had conversed without pause.

She felt exhausted, depressed, and almost unbearably homesick for the house at Kew and the life she had blithely discarded on what now seemed a most foolish impulse.

Again she woke up very early when everyone else was asleep. Fortunately her window was screened so that when she switched on the lamp it brought no invasion of insects.

For an hour she read a favourite book, and then fell asleep to wake at a more normal hour, and in a mood very different from her gloom of the night before.

Perhaps it was all part of jet-lag, that descent into uncharacteristic despondency. This morning she felt her usual self; prepared to make the best of the situation. If she had to forget about Lyle—so what? she told herself briskly.

She was still on a beautiful island, with an interesting job to engage her energies, and perhaps she would meet here the man whom Liz laughingly referred to as Mr Right. It would be typical of life's ironies if a girlish infatuation for Mr Wrong was the means to a happier end.

In this more sensible mood, she joined the Charbonnes for breakfast.

In the event, it was not Vashti who came to fetch her at ten, but a young, pleasant-faced West Indian who introduced himself as Jeff Glover, one of her editorial colleagues.

Enquiries about each other's backgrounds kept the conversation going for the first ten minutes of the drive. Jeff, a

Nevisian by birth, had learnt his job on various papers and, more recently, in local broadcasting. He could double as a reporter or sub-editor. He wasn't married and, like her, he was living in digs, with the difference that his landlady was a widow who went out to work and didn't cook meals for her lodgers.

'I eat out, which is more expensive, but it also gives me more freedom,' he explained. 'Women get upset if you keep a meal waiting and, in our job, it isn't always possible to be home on time.'

In the back of the car was his snorkelling gear. When he discovered that Sarah had never indulged in this pastime, he offered to teach her.

'On an island like this you have to be keen on water sports of some sort or you'd go out of your mind,' he warned her. 'Especially someone from London. There's very little cultural life here. You have to make your own entertainments.'

The fact that they had just passed a herd of black and brown goats foraging by the roadside and, coming in the opposite direction, an old man perched sideways on a donkey who had lifted his hand to them with a countryman's friendliness, underlined that this was a far cry from the busy streets of south London or the middle-class suburbia of Kew.

Soon after, Jeff turned off the road. They began to bump slowly along a rocky dirt road bordered by thorny undergrowth.

'This is the road to the beaches on either side of Emerald Hill. Lyle is not as cut off as you might think. He has electricity and a telephone,' he said, indicating the poles which carried the cables. 'What I'd like is a room in his house. It's big enough for all of us to live there in a kind of non-hippy commune.'

'Don't you think that might lead to clashes—working together *and* living together?' she suggested.

'I don't see why it should. You wait till you see it. I'm sure you'll prefer it to the Charbonnes' bungalow.'

Presently the dirt road forked. At the point of divergence was a gateway, the two rusty iron gates standing open to allow Jeff's small car to pass into the dim green tunnel formed by an avenue of neam trees with intertwining branches.

When they re-emerged into sunlight they were in a wide grassy space in front of an old stone-block two-storey house embellished by upper and lower verandahs of ornate, lace-like, white-painted cast-iron.

Jeff parked the car in the shade of an ancient silk cotton tree, and they crossed the grass to the opening in the balustrade of the lower verandah. It was unfurnished, as was the wide hall which led through from the open doorway to another at the rear of the house, with a graceful staircase curving up to the first floor.

'I expect they're all on the terrace,' said Jeff, referring to the occupants of several cars parked before his.

As he spoke a burst of concerted laughter came from somewhere beyond the rear doorway. Moments later they stepped outside on to a large, stone-paved terrace, partly shaded by trees growing through the spaces among the flagstones. Here, seated in a variety of beach chairs, were some of the lunch party and, with them, their tall, bronze-skinned host in a pair of white shorts.

'Hello, Jeff. 'Morning, Sarah. How are you? How was your first night with the Charbonnes?'

'Good morning. It was very comfortable, thank you.'

She knew then the complete futility of all her resolves before breakfast. There could never be anyone else while Lyle was a part of her life, even if he took no interest in her except as a member of his staff.

'Let me introduce you.' He kept a light hold on her arm just above the elbow as he told her the names of the others.

'Ray, our chief reporter, and his wife Hester'—indicating a couple in their early forties who murmured the usual civilities—'and Ted and Cleve who will set and print what you write, and Jimmy, our junior.'

The three males, the latter a youth in his late teens, stood up to shake hands with her.

Vashti, looking lovelier than yesterday in a kanga of pale blue voile knotted over a white bikini, with her hair flowing down to her waist, said, 'Hello, Sarah. I asked Jeff if he'd pick you up because I came over early to work for a couple of hours.'

She didn't look as if she had been working. Sarah couldn't help wondering if the truth was that she and Lyle were already lovers as well as colleagues, and he had persuaded her to spend last night at Emerald Hill. It would have been easy to ring Jeff and ask him to pick her up.

Not liking the thought, or herself for thinking it, Sarah smiled and determined to be friendly. Which wasn't difficult, for the other girl's personality seemed to be as pleasing as her looks. She seemed quite unconscious of her beauty. Her manner was that of a nice, unaffected girl with a tendency to sit quietly by while others talked, rather than expecting the limelight to be focussed on her ravishing looks as many beauties would have done.

From either end of the terrace flights of steps led down to the beaches, one a tiny crescent moon cove, and the other a half mile stretch of pale pink crushed coral sand with an amethyst-coloured shadow about fifty yards offshore indicating the presence of submerged reef.

'We'll have coffee, and then we'll swim,' Lyle told the two newcomers. 'I'm just going to the kitchen to see if Amy needs any help.'

He reappeared five minutes later, carrying a tray of assorted mugs and cups and saucers, and accompanied by a woman whom he introduced as Ted's wife, Amy.

Cleve, Sarah gathered, was unmarried; and the attention which he and Jeff paid to her, and their apparent lack of interest in Vashti's superior attractions, confirmed to her that they knew the other girl belonged to Lyle and there was no point in either of them pursuing her.

About two o'clock they had a take-away lunch in the large, lofty, fan-cooled dining-room where, at present, the furniture consisted of two planks laid across tea chests and the deck chairs brought in from the terrace.

Afterwards, Lyle asked Sarah if she would like him to show her the rest of the house.

She accepted eagerly, thinking Vashti would accompany them. But the other girl stayed downstairs, talking to Amy, while they climbed the staircase which had a balustrade like those of the verandahs except that it was capped with a mahogany handrail.

There were ten bedrooms, six with sea views and four overlooking the forecourt. Between them were dressing-rooms and large, walk-in closets which Lyle meant to convert into bathrooms.

He was sleeping in the only piece of original furniture still left in the house; a huge four-poster bed shrouded in folds of mosquito netting. He had improvised bookshelves with planks supported by bricks, and an old kitchen table of scrubbed deal was serving him as a desk.

'This house needs lots of antiques. Will you be able to buy any here?' she asked, as they stood on the balcony on the seaward side of his bedroom.

'They may take some hunting out, but I think so. The first thing is to get the place painted, and I'm hoping all of you will help me with that job.'

'I'd be happy to help. It's a lovely old place, and it'll be interesting to see it gradually restored to its former glory. When you've put it in order, it should be one of most beautiful houses in the West Indies.'

With one of the most beautiful girls in the Caribbean as

its mistress—that is if you marry her, she thought.

'What's the matter? Feeling homesick?' he asked her suddenly.

'No, I wasn't thinking about home.'

'Then why the forlorn look?'

'I—I don't know. I wasn't thinking forlorn thoughts,' she answered untruthfully. Then, turning away from the balustrade, 'You haven't shown me the rest of the ground floor yet.'

The drawing-room was like a small ballroom, with tall glazed double doors opening on to one end of the terrace. Here there were the original light fittings; tarnished silver sconces for candles with tulip-shaped clear glass shades. Lyle planned to convert them to electricity. Although the house had been wired by a previous tenant, each room had only one central hanging light and some socket outlets for plugs.

The only part of the mansion which Sarah did not like was the kitchen wing. This was a squalid reminder that the occupants of the house in its heyday had enjoyed their gracious, leisured lives at the expense of the female servants who had toiled in these smoke-blackened quarters for the same long, back-breaking hours that their menfolk had slaved in the cane-fields.

When she said this to Lyle, he shrugged, 'Exactly the same thing applies to all the great houses in England. White people who feel guilty about slavery tend to forget that in Europe there were millions of white slaves. They weren't called slaves, but that's what they were in practical terms. I've talked to old ladies in England who, after some rudimentary schooling, went into domestic service in the early years of this century. They had to get up at five on cold winter mornings to black-lead grates and light fires while their employers were asleep. They deserve our pity as well, you know.'

Sarah was struck by the breadth of his humanity. He was like her father on that score. There was nothing narrow about his mind.

He said, 'I haven't mentioned it to the others yet, but I'm thinking of offering them rooms here. Not on a permanent basis, but for the paper's first year. Ted and Amy are paying a high rent for a not very good furnished place, but they don't want to start buying a house until their future is more settled. Cleve, Jeff and Jimmy are in lodgings, but would be more comfortable here.'

'Jeff did mention, as we were coming, how much he would like a room here. But I thought it might create problems.'

'I've no doubt it will. But none that can't be resolved with goodwill and common sense—or by the person in charge, myself,' he added dryly. 'As you'll discover when you start working for me, I'm not a tyrannical taskmaster, but neither am I too easygoing. The *Independent* will be a team effort, but every team needs a captain to exert authority when necessary.'

'Is that a veiled warning? Do you suspect me of insubordinate tendencies?' she asked lightly.

He laughed. 'No, I don't think you'll give me any trouble, Sarah Mary Jane.'

He must have seen her second and third names when her passport was being checked at the immigration desk in Antigua. His use of all three made her feel about fifteen years old.

She was tempted to make a deliberately provocative response, then she remembered Vashti. She had always thought it contemptible to poach on another girl's preserves. Not that she was capable of filching Lyle from his gorgeous secretary. But had the situation been reversed; had she been the beauty and Vashti the ordinarily passable one, she would have disdained to flirt with him unless he was free and unattached.

So she said only, 'What does your initial R stand for?'

'Richard, after my father. He and my mother were killed when he was piloting his own plane and the engine failed. But I didn't want to tell you that the other morning when we were about to fly here in a small plane.'

'Oh, that was the reason you——' She left the remark unfinished.

'Sounded brusque?' he suggested. 'Yes, too brusque for someone of your sensitivity. I could see you thought I'd snubbed you. You aren't adept at hiding your feelings.'

His eyes were quizzical as he said this, his tone one of gentle raillery—again as if she were very young.

'Perhaps not,' she said, with spirit. 'But you needn't think I'm so sensitive that I'll wilt if you blast at me in the office. Bob could rant and rage, when he chose. Everyone had an occasional tongue-lashing, including me. I may have looked rather weepy when I said goodbye to my parents, but as a journalist I'm quite tough, I assure you.'

'Yes, indeed: well on the way to becoming one of those chain-smoking, gin-swigging battleaxes left over from Fleet Street's great days who were still around when I was a junior reporter,' he said teasingly. 'Come on—time to swim again.'

With a casual hand on her shoulder, he steered her back to the main house to rejoin the rest of the party.

That evening Sarah wrote to her parents, using the red leather writing case which had been a parting presentation from Bob and her fellow reporters.

In a letter to Liz, she wrote—*I could have had two dates this evening. Both Jeff and Cleve* (whom she had already described) *offered to take me out to supper. But Mrs Charbonne was expecting me to eat here, and I'm still not completely over my jet-lag.*

About Lyle she wrote little, being unwilling to admit, even to Liz, that where love was concerned she had come on a wild-goose-chase.

Sarah's first month in Compostela passed amazingly swiftly. Lyle had expected the paper's first and second issues to be sell-outs. But it was the long-term sales and the advertising as much as the editorial content which would maintain the circulation figures which the *Independent* had to have to keep it alive and flourishing.

On this side of the enterprise, Lyle was aided by an inspired and persuasive advertising manager.

As his name suggested, Terence Kilkieran was an Irishman. His career had not been in newspapers, but in advertising agencies, including a top New York agency. He and Lyle had met at a time when premature health problems had caused his doctor to warn him that, unless he changed his life-style, he was likely to die in his forties.

'So I've come to this one-horse town, and I've given up smoking and drinking—but I'm damned if I'll give up pretty women,' he told Sarah, with an exaggerated leer, one day when they happened to be the only two of Lyle's team in the coffee shop round the corner from the waterfront offices of the *Independent*.

He was about Lyle's age; had been married and was now divorced; and proclaimed himself a devil with women. Sarah felt this was largely moonshine, but it reminded her of Lyle's remark about the local wolves starting to prowl— black and white.

But neither Jeff nor Cleve, although always trying to make dates with her, were in any way wolfish in their attentions, and she didn't think Terence was as much of a menace as he liked to make out.

Having sold his apartment in New York, he had looked at the properties for sale on the island, and decided to buy a boat to live on.

Sometimes, on Sundays, he sailed it round the coast to Emerald Hill to see how the painting was progressing. Sarah spent nearly all her free time with a paintbrush in her hand, as did the others with a vested interest in the place.

It was not a wearisome labour with the sea close at hand whenever they felt like a break, and Lyle's big refrigerator stocked with cans of beer and a big jug of pineappleade.

She had a double motive herself. She enjoyed helping to do up the mansion, and was glad of an excuse not to share the Charbonnes' evening meal. It wasn't that Susan wasn't a good cook; it was that her menus were guaranteed to fatten people, and Sarah didn't wish to put on weight. Her mother always used wholefoods, and she found it hard to adjust to white rice, and soft crustless bread, and the dumplings which accompanied all her landlady's soups and stews.

One night she was working at the house when there was a power cut. It wouldn't have mattered except that she happened to be alone there, having finished work earlier than the others and asked Lyle for the key, as was customary with whoever was going to arrive first.

She had known that Ray and Jeff were working that evening, but had thought that at least one of the others would have joined her before it grew dusk.

Even when darkness fell, she wasn't worried by her solitude until the instant when the power failed and the upstairs room where she was painting was plunged into sudden and total blackness. No moonlight came through the window because it had been threatening to rain, and even if the sky had been cloudless there was only a thin crescent moon that week.

She remembered Lyle speaking of power cuts, and saying there were several old candlesticks and the candles to fill them in a cupboard in the hall.

But to reach them she had to feel her way along the landing, down the staircase and across the hall. Suddenly the old house seemed very eerie, and very isolated at the end of its cavernous avenue of trees, half a mile from the road and two miles from the nearest village.

Shutting her mind to thoughts of how many people had died there in the two hundred years since it was built, and to tales she had heard about jumbies, the restless spirits of those who had lived evil lives or met a violent death, Sarah forced herself to find her way to the door by moving along the wall with her fingertips on it.

By the time she had descended the staircase, her nerves were stretched taut by the horrible feeling that at any moment there might be an unearthly howl from some-where in the empty building, or that she would feel the cold draught which was said to signal the nearness of a jumby.

It was not going to be much better when she had a candle alight. The flickering glow, the feeling that she could be seen by watchers lurking in the shadows, might be worse than this dense, smothering darkness.

The sound of a car approaching sent a wave of relief coursing through her. Who was coming? Lyle or Cleve? Or perhaps Ted and Amy bringing Hester with them.

Sarah didn't care who it was as long as it was another human being, and not one of the supernatural presences she had seemed to feel near her seconds before.

Instead of going to the cupboard, she felt her way to the front door. As she opened it, the car's headlights illuminated the façade of the house. It stopped with its bonnet pointing towards the front door so that, dazzled by the twin beams, she could not see which car it was or how many people were in it.

Then Lyle's tall figure moved in front of the vehicle and was lit up for two or three seconds before he became sil-houetted as he walked towards her.

'Couldn't you find the candles?'

'I was on my way to the cupboard when I heard you coming. I was upstairs, you see, when the power failed. It took time to find my way downstairs.'

'You're alone here?' he asked her sharply.

'Yes.'

'Weren't you alarmed?'

'No, why should I be?' she replied, with an air of surprise.

He was mounting the steps to the verandah, and she was standing on the threshold of the right-hand side of the double doors. The left door was bolted in place and now, in the darkness behind it, something moved and made a strange noise.

Sarah gave a small smothered shriek and flung herself into Lyle's arms.

They closed round her, strong and secure. After a moment he said, 'It's only an extra large land-crab. He must have got shut in some time. Look, there he goes— perfectly harmless.'

She heard the rapid scuttling of claws and peered at the strange, stalk-eyed creature which had followed her out of the door and was beating a sideways retreat. She shuddered, clutching Lyle's shirt.

'So you weren't at all scared, eh?' he teased. 'Poor Sarah, I'm sorry about that. If I'd known you were here on your own I'd have come home before it got dark.'

'I was only a little bit nervous,' she murmured, ashamed of her panic.

'You're trembling as if you'd been terrified. Or is that at being in my arms?'

She would have withdrawn if she could, but his arm was clamped firmly round her.

His other hand tilted her chin up. 'Are you scared of me, Sarah?' he asked her.

'Of course not! Lyle . . . please . . . let me go!'

'In a moment.'

His voice had thickened. His head bent. He kissed her mouth.

CHAPTER FIVE

A THOUSAND times, in her teens, Sarah had imagined this kiss: herself caught in this man's arms, his lips hard and fierce upon her lips.

But it wasn't like that in reality. Lyle held her encircled with one arm, and the fingers which had tipped up her chin slid caressingly along her jawbone, past the soft place beneath her ear, and round to the nape of her neck.

His mouth was gentle on hers; warm, soft and infinitely tender, as if she were a young girl, and this was her first embrace, and he had to go cautiously with her.

Yet within him she felt the same blaze which had flared up in Roddy the last time he brought her home; the same sudden pounding of his heart, the same involuntary reaction of his big, strong, muscle-armoured frame to the contact with her feminine softness.

Roddy's passion had flared in the kiss from which she had shrunk. Lyle's ardour was leashed and controlled. He even slackened his hold so that she should be less aware of the hot desire pulsing in him.

He wanted her, she realised exultantly. He wanted her there and then, and she wanted whatever he wanted—to be carried upstairs to the four-poster bed in his room, to be undressed, to be made love to.

Her whole body tingled and trembled. She slipped her arms up round his neck, and pressed against him, instinctively parting her lips.

He lost control then—or nearly. The sudden yielding of her mouth, the implicit surrender of her body acted like a draught on the heat which was smouldering in him. His hand cupped the curve of her head as his lips became more demanding, and the arm round her crushed her to him. Locked together, they kissed in a way which made Sarah dizzy with longing.

Her senses, she found, had been only half awake until now. Unimagined frissons of pleasure spread slowly along her quivering nerves. Unknown instincts prompted her response to the long, sensual, unsparing kiss which seemed to go on for ever.

Then, all at once, it was over.

She heard him say hoarsely, 'Someone's coming.' Then, lifting her, he moved the few paces which took them inside the house.

In the darkness of the hall, hidden from his own head-lamps and those of the car arriving, he gave her another swift kiss and, as if he knew she was giddy and weak with emotion, pushed her close to the wall before he left her.

Sarah was grateful for its support as she strove to pull herself together. She heard the car stop, then voices. She knew she wasn't ready to face people, but where could she hide until her breathing had steadied, until she was no longer trembling?

At that moment two things happened. At the other end of the hall Lyle struck a match to light a candle; and, almost at the same instant, the power returned, causing a whoop from the new arrivals as they saw the lights go on upstairs.

Like the mongooses which lived in the garden and came for the scraps Lyle put out for them, darting swiftly away if a human appeared, Sarah fled up the stairs to the landing. In the sanctuary of one of the newly intalled bathrooms, she locked the door and listened to the voices from the hall. The house still being sparsely furnished, with nor curtains and rugs to absorb sound, conversations carried more clearly than they would when the place was in order.

'Hi, Lyle. The lights were off in the village when we came through so we knew you'd be in darkness here.

How long did the cut last?'

'Not long. I've only just arrived myself.' His voice sounded calm, and there would be no smudges of lipstick to betray what had happened between them because she was not wearing any.

'Sarah's car is outside. How long has she been here?'

'I'm not sure. An hour or two, maybe.'

'She was here on her own when the power failed? Wasn't she scared? I should have been.' This was Amy speaking.

'Sarah's an intelligent girl. She doesn't believe all that nonsense about jumbies like you do,' she heard Ted tell his wife, to take a rise out of her.

'I do not believe it,' she protested. 'And they have ghosts in England, you know—walled-up nuns and people who had their heads chopped off. I'm sure *you* wouldn't want to spend a night here, on your own with no lights.'

'Lyle sleeps here alone,' was his answer.

The remark was followed by a pause which reminded Sarah of someone she had forgotten while Lyle was kissing her. Vashti.

All the time she had been in his arms she had given no thought to the girl to whom he belonged, if not officially, morally.

Was there silence downstairs because Ted and the others knew that Lyle was not always alone at night? Sometimes Vashti stayed with him.

The rest of their conversation was less distinct as they moved from the hall to the room which he was having converted into a modern, air-conditioned kitchen.

Sarah went to the basin to wash her hands. Then if any of them came upstairs, they wouldn't guess she was using the bathroom as a bolthole.

The mirror reflected her face, and her face reflected the turmoil of the conflicting feelings inside her.

The arousing, for the first time, of the passionate depths

of her nature. The dismayed recognition of where those deep feelings might have led her had there been no timely interruption. The shame and resentment of finding that it had been an act of betrayal, by Lyle, and also by herself for forgetting Vashti's existence.

When Hester and Amy came upstairs, she was back at work, painting a skirting.

'Didn't you hate it, being here on your own in the dark?' Hester asked her.

'Yes, I did,' she admitted. 'Silly of me, I know, but there it is.'

She went home at the same time as the others and, when they were all saying goodnight, both she and Lyle behaved as if nothing untoward had happened.

The next night she had an assignment, and the night after that she let Jeff take her dancing at one of the hotels. The third night she stayed in her digs, writing a long letter home, and finishing a novel lent to her by Terence Kilkieran.

The following morning she went to his office to return the book to him. A few steps from the door, which was ajar, she heard a sound which she did not immediately recognise. The next instant the door was jerked open and Vashti hurried out. Her golden face was unusually flushed, and her dark eyes glittered with annoyance. At the sight of Sarah, she checked.

'*Men!*' she breathed, in a furious undertone, before she walked quickly away.

Staring after her retreating back, Sarah realised the sound she had heard had been the staccato smack of Vashti's palm striking Terence's face. She decided it was not the moment to give his book back to him.

Later, pondering the incident, she wondered if Vashti would tell Lyle that Terence had kissed her, or pinched her bottom, or whatever it was he had done to upset her. Since it didn't seem likely that he would deliberately tread on the toes of the man who was the paper's proprietor as well as its editor, she could only conclude that Terence was not aware of the relationship between Lyle and his beautiful secretary.

Later in the day Vashti came to the Reporters' Room and said, 'Lyle would like to see you in his office, Sarah.'

This was not an unusual summons because he would often call one or other of the reporters in to check a point with them, or explain some change he was making to their copy. But as it was the first time he had sent for her since he had kissed her, she felt a certain apprehension as she ran down the stairs to his office on the first floor.

'Come in, Sarah. Close the door, will you?' he said, as she entered his office.

He was writing as he spoke and did not immediately look up. In the office, but nowhere else, he dispensed with the courtesy of rising whenever his female staff came into his domain.

His instruction to close the door increased her trepidation. Normally it was always open. To see it closed was tantamount to a sign Do Not Disturb, and meant he had someone from outside the office with him.

'Sit down, please. I shan't keep you long.'

He took another few moments to finish the work he was doing before putting down his pen and leaning back in his chair.

After a full half minute of enduring his thoughtful scrutiny, she shifted uneasily in the chair on the other side of the desk.

'Is there something wrong with my coverage of the plans for the new children's clinic?'

'No. As always, your copy is impeccable. Shall we see you at the house this evening?'

'I—I don't think so. Not tonight.'

'You've a date, perhaps?'

'No, but I have . . . things to do.'

Lyle pushed back his chair and stood up. He came round to her side of the desk, and sat on the edge of it, arms folded, looking down at her.

'You're under no obligation to go on helping. You've done sterling service already. But I think I detect a certain constraint in your manner which must have to do with the last time you were at Emerald Hill. You're afraid of being kissed again, is that it?'

'I—I'm not afraid. I just don't want to be kissed again.'

'You appeared to enjoy it at the time.'

The mockery in his smile made her furious. 'And have regretted it ever since! If you have no compunction, I have. I happen to like Vashti. Frankly, I can't understand why, having someone like her at your disposal, you need any other cheap kicks. The fact is you don't deserve her. Now if you'll excuse me——'

But as Sarah would have sprung up and marched from the room, he said in a soft, steely voice, 'Sit still, Sarah. I haven't finished with you.'

She glowered at him, her mouth mutinous. But she dared not defy that quiet order to stay where she was.

'I'm sure you didn't work for Bob without hearing him repeat C. P. Scott's rule—Comment is free but facts are sacred.'

This was true: Sarah had frequently heard her previous editor quoting the man who had edited the second most famous English newspaper, the *Manchester Guardian*, in its heyday. But she could not see how the golden rule of all responsible journalists had any relevance at the moment.

'I imagine you also heard him thundering "You haven't checked your facts, boy," at the junior,' Lyle went on. 'So I'm rather surprised that checking isn't second nature to you—in your private as well as your working life.'

'What do you mean? What facts?' she said uncertainly.

'You appear to be under the impression that Vashti is

more than my secretary. What grounds have you for that assumption?'

She remembered her first sight of Vashti's beauty, and the other girl's glowing smile as she told him she was glad to see him back.

'I ... it just seemed obvious,' she faltered. 'She's so lovely, and you——' She stopped short.

'I am what?' he asked, with a snap. 'A man you don't trust much, clearly.'

Before she could answer, he went on, 'Vashti is engaged to a man who is training to be an hotelier at a resort in Florida. It isn't official yet because her family don't approve of him. They've been wealthy merchants for several generations, and he is the son of a taxi-driver. She has to cope with a lot of unwanted admiration because, as you say, she's beautiful. But she has no interest in anyone but Stephen. If you don't believe me, ask her.'

Sarah stared at him, temporarily tongue-tied. She saw now that there had been no concrete evidence to support her conclusion. It had been merely an inference based on what Rosemary had told her, and her feeling that he was a man who would always make a play for the most attractive girl in his circle and, nine times out of ten, would be successful because he was himself exceptionally attractive.

'However, there is one good reason why I shouldn't have kissed you the other night,' Lyle continued, his expression sardonic. 'The fact that we have to work together. But I gather that doesn't bother you, or you wouldn't have made a date with Jeff recently.'

'It wasn't a romantic date. We're both strangers here, living in digs, and we both like to dance,' she said quickly. 'We were colleagues spending an evening together. *He* didn't kiss me.'

'I expect he wanted to,' said Lyle. 'You'll have problems there, if you're not careful. He's a nice lad but not for you.'

She lifted her chin. 'How do you know?'

'If you were attracted by Jeff, you wouldn't have kissed me the way you did. Unless you're like that with all men, which I very much doubt,' he said dryly.

His telephone started to ring, and he stretched a hand to the receiver.

'Excuse me. Lyle Talbot.'

For some seconds, his eyes still on her, he listened to the voice on the line.

Then he said, 'Hold on a moment, would you?' and covered the mouthpiece with his hand. 'This is going to be a long call. We'll talk again later. Off you go, Sarah.'

Dismissed, she went back to her own desk, but not to resume writing up her notes about a new boutique for the women's page. Instead she sat staring absently at the keys of her typewriter, conscious of an immense relief that Vashti was not Lyle's girl-friend as she had thought.

You wouldn't have kissed me the way you did. Remembering his reference to her abandoned response, she felt her cheeks burn. He must think her a very easy prey, a girl who yielded her lips so swiftly and eagerly. Yet if he wanted her, and she wanted both to learn about love from an expert, and to get him out of her system, why should she hold back and pretend a coolness she didn't feel?

Several days passed. Sarah went back to spending her evenings at Emerald Hill whenever she wasn't marked down in the diary. But although she saw a good deal of him, she was never on her own with Lyle, either at work or at the house. Their conversation in his office was not resumed. As the weekend came and went, and a new week began, her puzzlement increased.

One day she went to a village to talk to an elderly countrywoman for a series of interviews with the island's oldest inhabitants.

The old lady, Mrs Rudolph, was wizened and hard of

hearing, but still active enough to keep her two-roomed house tidy. Loneliness—she did not get on with her neighbours, and had no family living near—made her delighted to see Sarah. She talked almost non-stop for several hours.

As a girl she had been a laundress, since when she had outlived three husbands. To the last of them, Mr Rudolph, she had been married in a chapel, an occasion which had been photographed. The two previous men in her life had been common-law husbands, Sarah guessed. When Mrs Rudolph was younger, the islanders, although always great chapel-goers—it being their only entertainment—had not bothered much about marriage.

She had a photograph of her second husband to show, but not of her first, the young fisherman, killed in a hurricane, who had been the man she had loved.

It almost brought tears to Sarah's eyes to watch the wrinkled old face under the clean cotton head-tie recalling the long-ago past when she had been younger than Sarah and in love with a man who had been dead for fifty years, but was still alive in her memory.

She showed Sarah her cluttered bedroom. Fortunately one of the village shops was only a couple of doors away as Mrs Rudolph was nervous of having her treasures stolen from her by the young men called Rastas who wore their hair long and appeared to do no work for their living.

As far as Sarah could see there was nothing there of any value. But outside, in an equally cluttered shed built by Mr Rudolph, there was one unvalued treasure.

Miraculously not much damaged, it was an eighteenth-century mahogany sideboard—perfect for the dining-room at Emerald Hill.

Lyle was not in the office when she returned, and she could not get to the house that evening because she was covering a meeting.

On a weekly paper, it was not necessary to write up night copy immediately, except the night before press day. But, living not far from the office, and still not wholly at ease among the Charbonnes, Sarah usually went back to the *News* building after her evening jobs.

She was still there at half past ten. This was late in St James, a town where, apart from two restaurants frequented by tourists, and a couple of discos patronised by the young, people tended to go to bed early.

All the editorial staff had keys, and when Sarah heard footsteps on the staircase she thought it was Ray who had also been working that evening.

But it was Lyle who walked into the reporters' room, looking surprised to find her there instead of his chief reporter.

'You're working late, Sarah. How come?'

'I've been writing up my interview with Mrs Rudolph. Lyle, she has the most beautiful sideboard stuck outside in a shed as a catch-all. It's in the style of a Sheraton piece . . . tapered legs, inlay, stringing. It's stunning. I told her about you, and asked her if she would sell it, and she was astonished that anyone should want to buy it. Could you go to see her tomorrow, before she changes her mind?'

For the moment her enthusiasm for the sideboard overrode all other considerations.

'By all means. How is it that you seem so knowledgeable about antique furniture? I don't remember your parents' house being furnished with it.'

'No, they only have some reproductions. I used to be friendly with a dealer who taught me to recognise the real stuff. When I have a house of my own I shall have nothing else. There's something about old furniture which has been used and polished for generations . . . oh, I can't explain it. You either like it or you don't.'

'As it happens I do,' he answered. 'I have seen some old houses furnished, and very effectively, with modern stuff, but it isn't my personal taste.' He glanced at his watch.

'Have you much more to do?'

'No, I was finishing as you came up the stairs. I'd better be getting home, Mrs Charbonne will wonder where I am.'

'Are you on foot tonight?'

'Yes. As the meeting was in the centre of town, I walked.'

'I'll walk you as far as your gate,' he said. 'There's a group of youths on the corner who might cause you some embarrassment.'

Did he really think that, or was it a pretext to re-open the conversation cut short in his office? But if he wanted to do that, why not here, in the office? Ray wasn't likely to come into the office at this hour. He was probably writing up his notes in the greater comfort of his home.

'It's kind of you,' she said uncertainly. 'But I doubt if they'd go beyond whistles and cheeky remarks. Where is your car?'

'It's parked at the top of the town. I've been strolling about, looked at buildings. It's easier to stand and stare at this time of night. Then I noticed the light on up here and thought I should find Ray at work.'

'I'm sorry it was only me,' she said, with a hint of coquetry.

A slight smile curved the well-cut lips. 'I'm not.'

As she stood up, he took in the dress she was wearing, a new one of rose-pink cotton. It wasn't a strappy sun-dress because she thought covered shoulders more suitable for her working hours. But in some ways it was more alluring than the bare-topped but loose-fitting dresses she wore when off duty. This had a bodice which clung to the shape of her figure, a waistline defined by a belt, and the kind of flared skirt that men liked, sleek on the hips but full and swirly at the hem.

Professionally observant as Lyle was, she doubted if to-morrow he would be able to describe what she was wearing tonight, except perhaps to remember the colour. It was the body inside the dress which he was appraising, in a way which reminded her of the definition of a successful dress as not the one admired by a woman's friends but the one which made her husband want to take it off.

Conscious of tremors inside her at the mere thought of being undressed by Lyle, Sarah reached for her bag and crossed the room to the door, leaving him to switch out the lights as he followed her downstairs.

The group of youths near the street corner did stare at her as she passed, but the presence of the man beside her— as tall and formidable as the town's police sergeant whose appearance was enough to quell the most bolshie young troublemaker—prevented them from uttering any comments, even in undertones.

'Careful!' Lyle put his hand on her elbow when the pavement ended at a deep gutter.

But he broke the brief contact as soon as she had stepped safely across it.

As they walked through the streets to her digs, well lit in places, shadowy in others, Sarah wondered if he wanted to kiss her again as much as she wanted to be kissed. He had said there was one good reason why he shouldn't have kissed her in the first place—because of their professional association. But she didn't think that would stop him if he wanted her.

A more insuperable obstacle was the lack of a place where they could be alone together. She could not invite him into her bedroom at the Charbonnes' house because it was solely a bedroom where even she could not sit comfortably in an armchair, but had to lie on the bed if she wanted to read. Emerald Hill offered little or no privacy. Except on that one occasion when the power had failed, invariably at least one of the others was there, and soon several of them would be sharing the house with him.

If only I had a place of my own, Sarah thought. Then I could invite him to dinner. It would all be so easy.

At a corner not far from the Charbonnes' gate, where a

group of trees made a patch of gloom, Lyle checked his stride.

'I'll turn off here. Goodnight, Sarah.'

She turned to face him. 'Goodnight. Thank you for walking with me.'

'My pleasure.'

For a long moment he looked down at her, and she stood with her face raised to his, feeling certain it was in his mind to take her in his arms. But evidently he thought better of it. Repeating his goodnight, he turned away down the road which would lead him to where his car was.

For a moment or two she watched him, admiring his lithe, easy carriage, disappointed by his failure to kiss her. Had she had a small flat she could have asked him in for coffee, and experienced again the sensual delight as his mouth came down firmly on hers.

As she turned towards the Charbonnes' gate, she had a deflating conviction that Lyle was unlikely ever to make a public date with her. Any private relationship between them would be just that—private. Not furtive, but extremely circumspect.

Which meant that as long as she lodged with the Methodist minister and his wife there would never be anything more between them than there was at the moment, one long kiss and a short one.

The problem was that there were no flats in St James and, if the planners were sensible, there never would be as they would be completely out of keeping with the style of the town and the housing needs of its inhabitants. There was no shortage of houses to rent, but only at the very high rates geared to wealthy tourists escaping from winter in the north.

Yet surely there must be somewhere she could have the privacy necessary for a discreet liaison with her editor. In that rôle Lyle, too, had his reputation to guard.

A few days later she was looking in a shop window when a

hand came to rest on the small of her back, and a voice said, 'How about a cold beer or a Piña Colada?'

She looked over her shoulder. 'Hello, Terence. I'd love a cold drink. As a matter of fact I've been meaning to ask your advice.'

'Then we'll find a secluded table in the Sugar Bird, and you shall have it, mavourneen.'

His hand still at the back of her waist, he began to steer her the short distance to a restaurant with a shady garden which was a popular rendezvous for tourists and residents.

As they settled themselves at a table under a canopy of leaves and he gave their order to a waitress, Sarah was amused to notice that Terence, as usual, was wearing a blue shirt which exactly matched the colour of his eyes.

They were his most striking feature with their vivid irises, and had they belonged to a girl naturally she would have dressed to accentuate them, as Sarah herself sometimes dressed to her black-lashed amber eyes. But she felt it was not quite the same for a man always to wear cornflower blue shirts.

'So what's your problem?' he asked her.

'I know that before you bought your boat you investigated other sorts of accommodation. I want to find a place of my own, and I wondered if you could suggest where I might begin looking.'

'You're not happy with your present digs?'

'They're fine—in some ways, not others. I'd prefer to cook for myself, or eat out if I was pressed for time. The Charbonnes eat so much stodge. I've put on three pounds in a month.'

'It suits you, honey.'

'But another three won't. Also I'd like to be able to entertain in a modest way, which I can't while I'm living chez Charbonne.'

'No, it must cramp your style in that respect,' he agreed.

'How d'you fancy renting a cabin aboard *Mazinga*? I
wouldn't object to you giving parties.'

She smiled and shook her head. 'This isn't London,
Terence, where men and girls share a flat and nobody
raises an eyebrow,' she answered lightly.

'No, I guess you're right. It's a pity. I think you'd like life
afloat, and there's plenty of room for two people to live on
Mazinga without a surfeit of togetherness. But this is a
straitlaced place compared with London or New York
where nobody bats an eyelid at the way other people
choose to live.'

And half the inhabitants don't care if their neighbours
drop dead either, was Sarah's unexpressed thought.

She was finding she liked island life, and the country
town atmosphere of St James. That she was prepared to
flout her parents' conventions by having a love affair with
Lyle didn't mean she was ready to cast aside all restraints.

She knew herself to be basically a conservative. Her
liking for antique furniture, representational paintings,
simple undating clothes, and one gold chain rather than a
boxful of junk jewellery, were all facets of a conventional
nature. She was not unadventurous, but nor was she a
rebel.

In fact she still wasn't at ease with the idea of taking a
lover. But if those were the only terms on which Lyle was
likely to want her, then she hadn't much choice. She could
never marry anyone else as long as his spell was upon her.

Unaware that she wasn't listening, Terence was talking
about the places he had considered before opting for his
present home. Sarah began to pay attention. The most
promising, by the sound of it, was a tiny house on the edge
of town.

'What put you off it?' she asked.

For a moment or two he hesitated, as if the reason had
slipped his mind. Then he said, 'It was rather cramped for
me, and the neighbours on both sides seemed to have large

numbers of children. I may be Irish, but I'm not in favour of kids everywhere. It may have been sold by this time, but I shouldn't think so. It's in a neighbourhood where most of the houses are rented, and although the price of this one is very low compared with the cost of holiday houses for non-islanders, I should think if anyone had the money to pay for it, they'd prefer to make a down payment on a place in a better class area.'

Before they returned to the *News* office, Terence introduced her to the agent who held the key to the property. Both men offered to take her to see it, but Sarah preferred to view the place on her own.

She went to see it that evening, going on foot, which was just as well because the street it was in was a narrow footway between the gardens of the houses on either side. None of them had any garaging for vehicles larger than motorbikes. It was a poor people's area, and some of the houses were slummy. Others were neat and well kept, with clean net curtains at the windows and orderly gardens with fences.

It was a locality where Sarah would not have been surprised to see people fetching water from a communal stand-pipe. But she knew from Terence and the agent that it had been among the first areas to receive mains water under a government programme to give all parts of St James the amenities of a modern capital.

The house was strawberry-ice pink, with the shutters and the pillars of the porch picked out in turquoise and white. It had a corrugated iron roof which would make it noisy when rain fell. But in Compostela the rain fell in short heavy showers, not days of unceasing drizzle.

Sarah opened the garden gate and walked up the path to the porch. Inside there was one fair-sized room and two small ones. In her mind's eye she saw them converted to a bed-sitter, a kitchenette and a shower with an indoor lavatory. Drainage was to a septic tank, and at present the privy

was outside, a hut in the garden screened by a banana
bush.

Some days later, Lyle summoned her to his office. He was
standing by the window when she entered. As he swung to
face her, she could tell he was extremely displeased.

'What's this I hear about you leaving the Charbonnes'?'
he demanded, frowning at her.

CHAPTER SIX

HAD Terence mentioned it? He was the only person in the office who knew she was moving, although the Charbonnes themselves knew, as did various people concerned with the sale.

'I was hoping to surprise you with an invitation to my housewarming. Who stole my thunder?' Sarah asked lightly.

'George Charbonne rang me up a few minutes ago to tell me you are leaving them, and they feel some concern about your plans.'

'Their concern is quite unnecessary,' she answered. 'I know what I'm doing—I'm the daughter of a lawyer, remember. The pitfalls of buying property are not a closed book to me.'

'Does your father know what you're doing?'

'If he's received my last letter—yes. But, in case you've forgotten, I am of age. I don't have to ask my parents' permission for my actions—or for the funds to finance them,' she added. 'I've arranged a loan from my bank. If the manager finds my intentions satisfactory, I don't know why the Charbonnes should fuss. I suppose it's because they're rather bourgeois in their outlook, and they wouldn't want to live in the district where my house is.'

'I'll reserve my own judgment on that until I've seen it. If you've nothing urgent on hand, you can take me there now.'

'But I don't want anyone else to see it yet. Not until my housewarming,' she protested.

'Without my approval, there won't be a housewarming,' was Lyle's rejoinder.

Sarah began to lose her temper. She felt furious with

George Charbonne for interfering, and upset that Lyle's reaction was the reverse of the one she had hoped for.

'You may be my boss. You're not my keeper,' she said hotly. 'If I choose to buy a house here, it has nothing to do with you. Your approval doesn't enter into it.'

'Does it not?' he said grimly. 'I've no doubt your loan was granted on the strength of your agreement with me. The bank may decide to withdraw it if I make it clear that it doesn't have my approval.'

'I've never heard anything so outrageous! What right have you to intrude in my private life?'

'The right of someone who promised your parents to keep an eye on you. There's no need to blow your top. Save your anger until I've seen the place.'

Grasping her by the arm, he propelled her briskly to the door, which he opened for her.

All the way down the stairs, and across the street to where his car was parked, Sarah quivered with suppressed indignation.

'Presumably we shall have to borrow the key from the agent who's handling the deal?' he said, as he unlocked the nearside door.

Coldly Sarah told him where to go, and sat silent and unrelaxed while he drove the short distance to the agent's office. There was little doubt in her mind that he was capable of quashing her plans if he chose. Considering that her ownership of the house was as much to his advantage as her own, she did not take kindly to being treated like an irresponsible teenager.

She did not speak again, except when it was necessary to direct him. Walking the last part of the way, she was much more conscious than on any of her several previous visits of the houses with neglected gardens and shabby façades.

None of her nearest neighbours had badly-kept homes. But she knew Lyle would not have missed the shaggy-

haired youth sitting on the steps of a porch in the same
street, listening to a transistor radio and looking suspici-
ously vacant-eyed. She had never seen him there before,
and silently cursed him for being there today.

But the fact that the street included one pot-smoking
layabout with dirty dreadlocks did not put her off it.
Coming towards them at this moment were two schoolgirls
in powder blue uniform pinafore dresses over blue and
white checked cotton blouses, their hair dressed in neat
corn rows, white teeth flashing as they chattered, immacul-
ate socks looking whiter by contrast with ebony legs.

'Someone must be making sacrifices to send those two to
a private school,' she remarked, in case Lyle should have
noted the youth but ignored the schoolgirls.

The small house seemed even smaller when he was in it.
His face revealed nothing of his thoughts as he looked at
what little there was to see. Then he began to ask questions;
the questions her father would have asked, and which she
had asked on her own account.

He asked none that she couldn't answer. As she had told
him, she was not a lawyer's daughter for nothing. She knew
about ancient lights, liens, leaseholds and searches. Not
that buying a pink-painted house, somewhat smaller than
her parents' garage, in the cheapest part of St James, was
like buying a property in England.

Even so she had done her homework before making up
her mind. Probably it was because she had all the facts at
her fingertips, and had already worked out the interest
charges on the loan she wanted, and how soon she could
pay it off, that her bank manager had acceded to her
request.

But would Lyle's reaction be equally favourable? Of that
she was even less certain than she had been of the outcome
of her visit to the bank.

'The loan will cover the cost of necessary improvements,

and essentials such as a bed, a cooker and a refrigerator,' she said, answering before he asked it what she thought must be his final enquiry.

There could surely be nothing else he would want to know after the exhaustive catechism of the past few minutes, she thought crossly.

'And you'll also need a good fire extinguisher,' said Lyle. 'These timber-built places are a fire hazard.'

For some seconds it didn't hit her that the remark implied his approval.

'You mean you *don't* object after all?' she asked warily.

He gave her a sardonic look. 'I've been accused of many faults, but never of being bourgeois. If you were unhappy with the Charbonnes, why didn't you say so?'

'I'm old enough to solve my own problems. You have enough on your plate.' Deliberately, Sarah made her tone distant.

She turned to the nearest window. The panes of glass opened inwards to allow the shutters to be closed from within the house. As she leaned out to pull them together, his strong hands closed on her waist.

The shutters met, darkening that side of the room. He turned her round, into his arms.

'When you're angry you look like a fierce little kitten,' he told her caressingly, before he kissed her.

For a few moments, still ruffled by his high-handedness, she tried to resist, to keep her lips closed and her body stiff, but she soon found it wasn't possible, any more than it was possible for a candle not to melt in the heat of the flame. Before the kiss ended she was clinging to him, her parted lips yielding to the hungry pressure of his mouth.

When he raised his head and slowly she opened her eyes, she felt dazed by the force of her response. It was like being caught unaware by a great white comber, and tumbled helplessly about in a turmoil of overwhelming emotions.

'I wasn't planning to do that, but you have an unfortunate knack of oversetting my good intentions,' Lyle said huskily, still holding her loosely embraced.

She could hear desire in his voice, and see it in his eyes. She felt it, too; a deep longing to surrender herself to him completely.

'Perhaps I won't have a housewarming party. There isn't really room for one, is there? A party *à deux* might be more suitable,' she murmured provocatively, her hands moving lightly on his broad shoulders, her eyes on the dent in the centre of his uncompromising chin.

'Is that an invitation?' he asked.

Had the question a double meaning? Was it an oblique way of making her confirm or deny the promise in her previous remark?

'Yes,' she said boldly. 'Yes, it is. But I can't fix the date at the moment. I don't know how long it will take to make the place ready.'

He released her and walked away to deal with the other shutters.

'Not long, I imagine,' he said to her, over his shoulder. 'I suspect that shortly my work force will transfer their efforts elsewhere. Not that it matters. The redecoration of my house is almost complete now.'

'I shall repaint this house myself. It's too small to need a team of people.'

'Just so long as you don't overdo it. All work and no play isn't good for anyone.'

Lyle had finished closing up the house. Now he strolled to where Sarah was waiting to re-lock the door, and brushed her cheek with his knuckles.

'I shall hold you to that invitation. A dinner for two. Can you cook?'

'Not as well as my mother, but quite well.'

For a moment longer they stood in the empty room, exchanging glances. The message in her eyes was *I love you*, but she doubted if he read it correctly. The message in his

was clear: he wanted to make love to her with the fierce
urgency of a virile man who, for reasons to do with his
position, had probably abstained from anything which
could attach gossip to him since their arrival on the island.

During the time she had misunderstood his relationship
with Vashti, she had not paused to consider how damaging
to the paper it would be if its editor was considered to be a
man of loose morals by the strait-laced members of the
Government, the Chamber of Commerce, and other influential groups.

Accustomed to living in London where, as in every great
city, all kinds of illicit activities passed unremarked, even
by neighbours, she had not realised how impossible it
would be for a liaison between the daughter of a leading
merchant family and the editor of the newspaper to remain
unnoticed.

On the other hand, if the editor and a member of his
staff, not an island girl, chose to carry on a discreet affair,
that would be a different matter. Particularly if their love
nest was in a locality such as this where the residents,
although mostly respectable, were not among the leading
citizens.

Walking back to the car, they were silent. Sarah wondered what Lyle's thoughts were. How strange that half an
hour ago she had felt him to be an insufferable despot,
exerting his authority over her to an extent beyond bearing. Now all that was forgotten, erased by a kiss.

He put her into the car and walked round to the driving
seat. As he slid behind the wheel he said, 'After we've
returned the key, shall we pick up your beach gear and go
for a swim?'

'It would be lovely, but can you spare the time?'

The thought of being alone with him on a secluded
beach sent ripples of excitement along her nerves.

'A couple of hours? Yes, why not?'

The car glided forward. Lyle was a smooth, relaxed

driver. Sarah watched his hands changing gear and turning the wheel with the light easy movements of a man who, if he had any hang-ups, didn't work them off by aggressive, competitive driving.

She thought of his hands on her body, touching her with the same confident expertise, and she started to tremble again.

Did he mean to make love to her today? Not to wait until her house was ready?

If that had been his intention, it was not to be realised. When, leaving him in the car while she went into the office to pick up her beach bag—which she always kept in the reporters' room in case there was a chance to swim during the day—she encountered Vashti on the staircase.

'You don't know where Lyle might be, do you?' his secretary asked her. 'Usually he leaves a note on his message pad if he's going to be out of the office for more than ten minutes.'

'I've just left him outside in the car. Is it anything urgent?'

'Yes. His sister has arrived unexpectedly. She's waiting for him in his room.'

Raine. Five foot eleven ex-model, married to a political journalist and living in Washington D.C. Favourite scent, Femme. Now retired and having babies.

As her memory retrieved the brief description of his sister given by Lyle during their flight from London, Sarah said, 'I'll run down and tell him she's here.'

'Would you? Thanks, Sarah.' Vashti began to ascend again.

Descending, Sarah knew that her reaction to the unexpected turn of events was a mixture of disappointment and relief. She wanted Lyle to become her lover, but not hurriedly, not in the shade of a sea-grape bush without the certainty of privacy.

He was not in the car but standing beside it when she rejoined him. Sometimes he wore well-pressed summer-weight trousers in light colours. Sometimes, as today, he wore white or pale khaki shorts with long socks, folded over below the knee, which showed off his ankles and calf muscles—although she didn't think he wore them for that reason, like Terence with his cornflower shirts, but because they were cool and comfortable. Whatever he wore, he always looked clean and spruce.

He smiled, reaching out for her beach bag to put it in the car for her. Was it the smile of a man who thought he was about to launch a casual affair with a girl he desired, but didn't feel a vestige of love for?

'Your sister is here,' she said flatly.

'Raine? Good God! Why didn't she wire me?' His out-stretched hand fell. 'I'm afraid this means the postpone-ment of our swim.'

'Never mind. What a nice surprise for you.'

'Come and meet her,' he invited.

'No, she'll want you to herself at first. I'll meet her later, I expect. Which reminds me, I need some toothpaste, and the shops will be closing in ten minutes.'

Smiling, Sarah turned away. The toothpaste was only an excuse. She needed a little breathing space before going back to what she had been doing before Lyle's summons.

The shops in St James closed at four. Strictly speaking, she needn't have gone back. But she had left her new library books on her desk, so she did go back, and found Raine holding court in the reporters' room, chatting to Ray, Jeff and Jimmy as if she had known them for months instead of minutes.

'And this is Sarah,' said Lyle. 'My sister . . . Raine Carpenter.'

'How do you do, Mrs Carpenter?'

Sarah looked up and Raine looked down, her unusual height elevated by the cork wedges of her mules. She was still an inch shorter than her brother, but she towered over everyone else until, having shaken hands and told Sarah not to be formal, she resumed her perch on a corner of Ray's desk.

She was not of the school of models who, seen in the street without make-up, their hair bundled up in a scarf, are almost unrecognisable as the greyhound-limbed beauties of the glossies.

Although retired, she was still as glamorous as her photographs. A fluid dress of thin cotton jersey, the colour of lettuce hearts, had brought her, cool and uncrumpled, from the United States to the islands. However, it was not what she wore but the perfection of her grooming and the beautiful proportions of her bones which made her striking.

Presently Lyle said, 'I wonder if you would do me a favour, Sarah? Would you run Raine out to Emerald Hill and help her to settle in?'

'Of course . . . with pleasure,' she said, puzzled.

He answered her unspoken question. 'I'm committed to dining with a Canadian couple who are only here for a few days. I can get out of the actual meal, but I want to talk to the husband on a matter of business. So I'll go and spend an hour or so with him, and then I'll be free for the rest of the evening.'

'I'm sorry to give you this trouble. I should have cabled,' said Raine presently, as Sarah drove her out of town. 'But Lyle's usual style is to arrive out of the blue, unannounced, so I thought I would do the same.'

'It's no trouble at all. To swim at Emerald Hill is a treat,' was Sarah's answer.

'Is it lovely, this house Lyle has leased?'

'I think so, and when it's finished, with curtains and paintings and flowers, it will be even more beautiful.'

'He wants my advice about curtains. You appear to have excellent taste,' said Raine, with a glance at the younger girl's pink cotton tee-shirt which had a motif on the sleeves repeated on the hem of her matching pink wraparound skirt. 'Do you think one can find decent fabrics on this little island, or will they all have to be imported?'

'I'm not sure. There are some very good dress fabrics if one pokes about for them, but I haven't looked for furnishing fabrics—although I shall now that I'm buying a house of my own.'

'You're buying a house? But you're not married, are you?' said Raine, looking startled.

'No, it's only for me . . . it's tiny. Rather like that one,' said Sarah, indicating a house they were passing which was about the same size as hers.

'How cute. But how come you need a house? You're not one of the people who are going to share Emerald Hill with Lyle?'

Sarah shook her head.

'I think he's mad,' said his sister. 'What's the point of leasing a place with plenty of elbow room and then filling it up with sub-tenants?'

'It's only for the first year, while the future of the paper is uncertain.'

'By then it may be hard to dislodge them, and his wife— if he's found one at long last—may not fancy sharing her home with several of his colleagues. By the way he writes, I think he's at last found a place to call home. Could you live here permanently? I doubt if I could.'

'Why not?' asked Sarah.

'Too small, too parochial, too limited culturally and socially.'

'But if your husband had wanted to do what Lyle is doing, you would have come with him, wouldn't you?'

'Yes, because theatres and galleries and amusing, stimulating dinner parties are very important to me, but Paul is *essential*,' said Raine. 'I'd be much worse off without him than without the other things I care about. But I should miss them a great deal. I shouldn't be as happy as I am

now. However, it isn't impossible—the adjustment from
my kind of life to this'—with a gesture at the rural landscape, cattle grazing on one side of the road, cotton growing on the other. 'I used to work with a photographer—
Norman Parkinson, you may have heard of him—who
moved from England to Tobago, and took to sausage pro-
duction there. Mind you, he didn't completely change
horses. He continued doing some photography and escaping every so often. And you can bet your bottom dollar that
Lyle will too, when the paper is established. He may have
found his place in the world, but he'll still want to have
periodic glimpses of the rest of it.'

Two hours later, when Lyle came home, he found them
strolling on the longer beach, Sarah in her apricot bikini
and Raine in a white one-strap one-piece, with her hair—
more silky than his—smoothed back into one thick braid.

He had taken off all but his shorts when he strolled
through the shallows to meet them, and the setting sun
burnished his torso and his long, powerful thighs. When
they were a few yards from each other, he produced a
camera from his pocket and moved to the back of the beach
to snap them against a background of the sea and the sunset
sky.

'Hold it, girls!' he instructed.

'Now our best profiles, if you please,' said Raine, when
the camera had clicked. 'Which is your best profile, Sarah?'
She took Sarah's chin in her hand, and turned her face this
way and that. 'Equally pretty on both sides, you lucky
creature.'

It was, Sarah knew, friendly flattery, to make her feel less
aware of being completely outshone by this beautiful, ele-
gant woman who seemed incapable of making an ungrace-
ful movement.

'Shall I take one of you and your sister?' she suggested,
when Lyle had snapped them a second time.

He handed over the camera, showed her how it functioned, and went to stand close to Raine with his arm round her waist. Together, they looked even more superb than they did individually; two tall, self-confident people who had both made their mark in the world, tasted fame and, finding it wanting, turned their talents to other objectives.

'Now I'll take one of you and Sarah for her to send home to her parents,' said Raine.

By this time Sarah knew all about Raine's three children, and Raine knew about the Grahams.

Lyle stood beside Sarah, not touching her, while his sister peered through the viewfinder. Being more expert than either of them, she was dissatisfied with what she saw.

'Without shoes on, Sarah is dwarfed. Can't you sit down or something?'

'How's this?' Lyle knelt on one leg and drew Sarah on to the other.

'Much better—good. Just a minute . . .' She came closer and knelt down herself. 'That's fine. No, wait—put your arm along his shoulders, will you, Sarah? That's marvellous . . . great!' The camera clicked twice. She stood up. 'Tomorrow I'll use the rest of this roll on shots of the house. It's gorgeous, Lyle. I adore it. But all those tall windows are going to cost a fortune to curtain. Maybe Roman shades are the answer.'

He rose to his feet. Sarah had sprung off his leg the instant the snaps had been taken. The intimate pose—more suited to an engaged couple than to an editor and his girl reporter—had reanimated the feelings he had stirred in her earlier that day.

'What are Roman shades?' he asked his sister.

'Oh, you know—those flat blinds with tapes which pull them up in sections, like a concertina. Or, better still, pulling-up curtains which are the newest window treatment in all the most chic period houses. What you need is that super book about decoration in eighteenth-century houses by the English designer John Fowler. As soon as I get back to Washington, I'll order a copy and send it to you. What a pity you haven't a wife to cope with the house while you're busy nursing the paper.'

Lyle ignored this remark. He said, 'As you're always dining out in Washington, I thought it would be more relaxing after your flight to have supper here. I stopped on the way home for roti.'

'Mm ... delicious! I remember having them before, when I was working in Trinidad,' said Raine.

Literally, roti meant bread, but in Compostela and many other Caribbean islands it had come to refer to the envelope-shapes of unleavened bread, rich with the clarified butter called ghee and filled with curried chicken or seafood, which people bought to take on picnics.

'I must be getting along or I shall be late for my supper,' said Sarah.

'I bought three rotis,' he told her, and forestalled her objections by adding, 'And I telephoned Mrs Charbonne to tell her you'd be eating with us. Also that I liked your little house and thought you'd be all right living there. I'm going to have a quick swim. Do you girls want to shower before supper?'

'I do. Salt water's so drying,' said his sister. 'Do you find that, Sarah? No, I guess at twenty-one I had no problems. But now that thirty is looming, I have to take greater care of myself.'

They left Lyle and returned to the house, exchanging girl-talk as easily as if they were old friends. For all her glamour, Raine was as comfortable to be with as Liz.

She came down to supper wearing a loose silk collarless tunic with the sleeves rolled up to mid-forearm, over a pair of close-fitting silk trousers which she told Sarah were called churidars. The tunic was aquamarine, the churidars pale olive green, and round her neck was a long rope of carved jade beads. The effect was both luxurious and casual.

When the crab-filled rotis had been reheated, she tucked a large napkin in the opening of her tunic and tackled her supper with the enthusiasm of a hungry child, dispensing with knife and fork and licking her fingers when she had finished.

Some day, Sarah thought wistfully, Raine Cárpenter was going to make a delightful sister-in-law for the future Mrs Lyle Talbot, wherever that fortunate person was waiting in the wings for her entrance into his life.

The evening passed swiftly, with much laughter and lively gossip about people connected with journalism. Raine told the others an anecdote concerning Clare Boothe Luce, once a war correspondent in China, and the second wife of Henry Luce, the American magazine millionaire. Apparently her jewels included a magnificent gold bracelet presented to her by the king of a well-known Arab state. It was said that, a man of extraordinary virility, he had had one hundred and fifty wives. But at one stage of his life he had been worried about impotence, and Mrs Luce had put him in touch with the person whose advice had cured him.

'The remedy—and it was successful—was to select one woman and be faithful to her for a year. For Mrs Luce's part in his cure, he gave her this fabulous bracelet,' said Raine. 'Do you think any man could really cope with all those wives?'

'I think this conversation is becoming too ribald for Sarah's ears,' said Lyle. 'It's time I ran her home. You won't need your car early tomorrow, Sarah. Raine can drive it in for you when she comes to look round the shops.'

'Oh, but——' she began.

'Don't argue, my child. You're not driving yourself back at this hour.'

Sarah glanced at her watch. 'Half past ten isn't late.'

'It's gone midnight. Your watch must have stopped.'

'And if you leave your car for me, Sarah, it means I can have a nice laze instead of having to be ready by whatever ungodly hour Lyle leaves for work,' put in his sister.

So it was that, not really unwillingly, Sarah submitted to being driven to St James by Lyle.

'What do you make of Raine?' he asked her.

'I wish she lived here,' she answered sincerely.

'If the *Independent* is successful, my brother-in-law might be interested in joining forces with me to revive the *Star* in Antigua.'

'I don't think your sister would like that. She said to me earlier on that living here wouldn't suit her, although she would be forced to do it if it was what her husband wanted.'

'How do you feel? Will a year in Compostela be about as much as you can stand?'

'No, I feel I could live here for ever—with occasional holidays away.'

'Mm, but you haven't been here two months yet. That's not long enough for the novelty to start wearing off.'

It was only a fifteen-minute drive. All too soon they were nearing Sarah's lodgings. Lyle stopped the car under the trees where he had said goodnight after walking her home from the office. The moonlight was brighter tonight, but this served to make the shadows darker by contrast.

Having switched off the headlights and the engine, he turned to her. 'Raine is here for six days. I can't take too much time off to be with her. I'd be grateful if you'd help to keep her company when I can't.'

'I'd be delighted.'

'Thank you.'

He slid his arm along the backrest until his fingers could touch the nape of her neck. So light a caress, yet it made her quiver with pleasure.

'Raine's visit will curb my style, which will be a good thing,' he said, speaking very quietly. 'It's dangerously easy to forget that you're one of an endangered species which I've always regarded as being under a preservation order.'

'You mean . . . virgins,' she said, very low.

'Precisely.' His fingers stilled on her neck, but they did not leave it.

'But the only reason I'm a virgin is because I never met anyone I felt sure would make the first time wonderful for me. You could do that, couldn't you, Lyle?' This last was a husky whisper.

She slid lower down on the seat, turning and tilting her head so that her cheek rested against his wrist. The side-lights gave out a glow which must reveal her face to him as it showed his to her. She looked at him with wide, expect-ant eyes, her earlier misgivings forgotten in the longing to be kissed.

'Oh, God!' His voice sounded ragged. Then he swooped like a hawk, and his lips seared her cheeks, her temples, the delicate curves of her eyebrows, the sensitive skin of her eyelids.

Their mouths met. Her lips parted at once, and her slim arms crept round his neck. Her fingers touched his crisp hair. She forgot that they were in a car, in a street, where they could be seen. She only knew she was with Lyle, in a wildly exciting sensual heaven.

Even when his hand searched the soft contours under the thin pink cotton her shudder was not a recoil. It was he who, at last, pulled away, a sound like a groan breaking from him.

For some moments he leaned on the steering wheel, and Sarah felt him struggling with himself. Then he opened his door and climbed out, and walked round the bonnet to her door.

'Out you come, Delilah.' Now his voice was controlled and sardonic.

In silence they walked to her gate which he unlatched and pushed open for her.

'Th-thank you for bringing me home.'

'Goodnight, Sarah.' His tone was clipped.

As he strode back towards the car, she had an uneasy feeling that he must be angry with her.

CHAPTER SEVEN

THE next day, as Lyle had been bidden to lunch with the island's Deputy Premier who was also the Minister of Economic Development and Tourism, Raine had lunch with Sarah in town.

'The Irishman, Terence Something, has asked us to supper tonight,' she said, when they had ordered chicken salads. 'What's he like, and what is his boat like?'

'Terence Kilkieran. He's nice . . . very quick-witted and amusing. The boat is called *Mazinga*, but I haven't been on board her.'

'Poor Lyle, how he must miss his boat,' said Raine. 'She was such a beauty; a sixty-foot cutter-rigged racer built for him at Hamble in England, where they've been building boats for six hundred years, would you believe?'

'I didn't know he'd had a boat,' said Sarah. 'What happened to her?'

'He had to sell her to raise the money to launch the paper. I don't know how much she fetched, but at least eighty thousand pounds. When he wasn't racing her, or cruising, he would let selected people charter her—only those who knew what they were doing; no bungling amateurs. *Thalia* was his darling, his love. He was as possessive and protective as other men are with their wives. I was astonished that he could part with her.'

'Why was the boat called *Thalia*?' asked Sarah, thinking, perhaps, to hear about one of his girl-friends.

'After one of the three Graces. Didn't you learn about them at school? They were Euphrosyne, Aglaia and Thalia, and they lived with the Muses on Mount Olympus and bestowed the gifts of happiness, kindness and charm on human beings. I forget who gave which, but Thalia's namesake certainly gave Lyle a great deal of happiness. He called her his hold on sanity. There's a lot of insanity in the life of a roving reporter. Not only the wars and disasters they have to cover, but the jockeying for power and all the pettifogging intrigues which go on behind the scenes in television. He's lost his beloved *Thalia*, but at least he's escaped from all that.'

'And he's doing something very worthwhile. When you think how few papers there are which don't print sensational rubbish, and pin-ups as sops to the half-wits, I think what he's doing is *immensely* important,' said Sarah earnestly.

'So does Paul. He believes Lyle has many fine qualities which are overshadowed by his tremendous charisma. My husband sees people in depth, not just as they seem on the surface. He's one of the few men who ever treated me as an intelligent woman and not merely a clothes-horse.'

Sarah would have been happy to encourage Raine to talk about her brother all through lunch. But she felt it would not do to show too much interest in him as a man as well as an editor. She changed the subject by asking what Raine had thought of the city's shops.

'Rather depressingly "small town", but I suppose I'm spoilt,' she conceded. 'I've been thinking about what I said to you on the drive out to Emerald Hill yesterday. I believe, if Paul ever did decide to opt out of the so-called rat race, maybe I could compensate by opening a boutique or even a health farm.'

When Sarah returned to the office she found a note on her desk. It was from the advertisement manager.

Lyle and Raine are coming to supper, and I'm hoping you can make it a foursome. 8 p.m. Dress: Casual. Terence.

After a short pause for thought, she walked down the

stairs to his office, opposite Lyle's.

When he called 'Come in,' she put her head round the door. 'I'd like to come. Thank you, Terence.'

'Great! In that case, come early, will you? I'll get hold of some flowers and you can arrange them for me. Say about half past seven. Okay?'

Sarah nodded. 'Okay.'

Thus it was that when the others arrived, she was already on board, wearing a plasticised apron to protect her dress and helping her host in the galley.

It wasn't until she and Terence, who had just been making her laugh at one of his tales of New York, heard a rapping on the coach-roof that they realised that the others had crossed the gangplank. And it wasn't until Terence called them below, and they all four converged in the saloon, that Lyle's slightly lifted eyebrow made her wonder if her being there before them, and the borrowed apron, suggested a greater degree of friendship with the Irishman than was actually the case.

Lyle had been out of the office most of the day, and it was the first time Sarah had seen him since the night before. Remembering the interlude in the car, and how it had been he and not she who had called a halt to the passionate kisses and caresses, she felt her cheeks starting to burn.

Did he think less of her for allowing so much licence last night? Would she rate higher in his opinion if she had been cooler, more elusive? Was he too used to girls who succumbed? Would the one who eventually won him be the one who held out for the longest?

Having organised drinks for everyone, Terence was curious to know what had passed between Lyle and the Deputy Premier. This was a matter of less interest to Raine than to Sarah—or perhaps she had heard it already—and presently his sister began a separate conversation about the curtains for Emerald Hill. Sarah was interested in this, too, but she would have preferred to continue listening to the men. However, politeness obliged her to give her attention to Raine's remarks.

Supper began with avocado pears, followed by a pizza with salad, followed by fresh fruit and cheese.

While they ate, Terence and Raine kept up an entertaining duologue about their experiences in New York. Lyle chipped in an occasional remark, and Sarah, having nothing to contribute, listened and laughed, and strove to appear undisturbed by his presence.

But it was very difficult, she discovered, to put on a carefree manner while seated close to a man who, a little more than twenty-four hours ago, had swept her to a pitch of abandonment which, had they been somewhere more private, might have led to the ultimate surrender. Not might—would, she corrected herself.

There were moments, during the meal, when she saw him glance round the saloon, and guessed it reminded him of his own boat, now the property of someone else.

They had coffee up in the cockpit which had cushions to convert the lockers into comfortable seats. Someone on one of the other boats was playing a guitar, and the trade wind was strumming the rigging of all the boats moored to the quay. In the moonlight, their aluminium masts looked like a grove of silver trees in an unearthly landscape painted by Frank Frazetta.

'Tell you what: the day after tomorrow being Sunday, why don't the whole bunch of us make a day of it and sail to one of the smaller, uninhabited islands?' suggested Terence. 'I'm told there's some fabulous snorkelling around Booby Island, and being a more expert helmsman than I am, Lyle, you could really put *Mazinga* through her paces.'

Raine said, 'That's a splendid idea. I'm a great barbecue cook. We'll buy lots of spare ribs and bangers, and if we can't muster enough cool boxes for the beer and the salad, I'll buy you a couple as a housewarming present, Lyle.

They're so useful to have in the car whenever you're food-shopping.'

It was agreed that, there being no events requiring cove-rage that Sunday, the entire newspaper staff should take part in a Caribbean-style wayzgoose, this being the English name for an annual dinner for employees in the printing trade or for newspaper staff outings.

When the supper party broke up, Lyle said, 'May we drop you off, Sarah?'

Before she could answer, Terence said, 'No, I'll see the girl safely home. I like a stroll last thing at night.'

'Thank you for a lovely evening, Terence, and I'll see you again on Sunday,' said Raine. 'Goodnight, Sarah. I shan't come into town tomorrow. I'm going to be gloriously lazy and spend the whole day in a hammock.'

Lyle thanked his host for the meal, and added briskly, 'Goodnight, Sarah.'

'Goodnight.'

Hurt and vexed by his unfriendly manner—his offer to drop her had been expressed in the tone of a no-nonsense parent speaking to an inclined-to-be-wilful teenager—she waited until the others had crossed the gangplank but were still within earshot, to say, 'I'll help you wash up, Terence.'

They went below and cleared the table. But with all the dishes neatly stacked, Terence said, 'I won't bother wash-ing up tonight. We'll have one for the road before I walk you home, acushla.'

She didn't think the Irish endearment was of any sig-nificance, or that he had it in mind to repeat whatever approach had provoked Vashti into slapping him. However, to be on the safe side, she said, 'No nightcap for me, thanks, Terence. If you don't want a hand with the dishes, I think I should be getting back now.'

'All right,' he answered amenably.

She felt sure she was not his type, any more than he was hers. Even if Lyle had not existed, she could never have had a close relationship with Terence. As well as the major reasons against it, there were any number of minor ones. She couldn't bear bitten nails, and also he had a thin mouth.

But not being attractive to each other didn't preclude them from having an amiable chat on the half-mile walk to her digs.

There was one small incident on the way which made her faintly uneasy but, with so much else on her mind, she didn't think about it for long.

It occurred when the quiet was disturbed by a car screeching round a corner at a speed which, had an elderly person been in the road at that moment, might have caused a serious accident.

'Stupid b—— bastard!' Terence exclaimed, as the driver, a youth, roared away with a smoking exhaust.

Sarah agreed with his sentiments, and had no objection to the force with which he expressed them. Her father's age and his upbringing made him refrain from strong language in the presence of his wife and daughter, and Mrs Graham greatly disliked bad language on television, and hearing the daughters of her friends using words which girls, in her youth, had not known, let alone uttered.

There were occasions, although not when her mother was around, when Sarah would mutter one of the milder expletives. But although she didn't use it herself, she was accustomed to hearing much cruder language and, in south London, 'bastard' was a commonplace, even, sometimes, a term of approbation.

What shocked her was the momentary impression that what Terence had almost ejaculated was *Stupid black bastard!*

And had he said that it would have repelled and alarmed her, as it would had she heard a black person say violently, *Stupid white bastard!*

Only a few days before she had heard Lyle talking to

Ray about some race riots he had covered within the past
year. On the whole his sympathies had been with the
rioters, provoked beyond bearing into their futile rampage.
But he had condemned without reserve the atrocity committed by one group of them. Unaware that Sarah was in
the small file room adjoining the reporters' room, he had
told Ray, in detail, what had happened. It had made her
feel physically sick to think of any human beings wreaking
such a horrible vengeance on a man for no better reason
than that he was of a different colour from the mob among
whom he had fallen.

The youth in the car, whether merely showing off or
high on drink or a drug, was indeed a stupid and dangerous
menace. But his colour had nothing to do with it; and in
that qualifying adjective was the germ of an insensate
hatred which could become an epidemic, and had done so
in the riots described by Lyle to his chief reporter.

However, by the time they reached her gate, she had
decided that she must have imagined the half-swallowed
adjective.

If Terence disliked black people, why take a job on an
island which now was governed by them and where, apart
from the floating population of tourists, people of European
stock were in the minority?

In Compostela, the predominant strain was a mixture of
Hausa, Fulani, Mandingo and Koromantee, and the predominant colour was brown in every shade from ebony to
café au lait.

As an expatriate Irishman, Terence must be especially
aware of the evil results of putting emotive labels on groups
instead of thinking of them as people. No, she could not
have heard what she thought she had heard.

The wayzgoose began at ten o'clock on Sunday morning
when everyone who worked for the *Independent*, including
Dudley, the new staff photographer, who had only been

with them a week; Gloria, the girl in the ground floor office who dealt with small ads and general enquiries, and Gary, the odd job boy, assembled on the quay.

Sarah was wearing a bikini and, over it, a pair of denim shorts and an American tee-shirt with a Kliban cat printed on the front. Several of the others had a tee-shirt with a slogan on it. Ted's bore the legend *My Wife Has A Drinking Problem—Me!* And Raine's shirt had a bunch of multi-coloured balloons and *Happy Birthday Boston*.

The writing on Lyle's shirt was almost illegibly faded. *Antigua Sailing Week 1977.* Sarah had heard about the neighbouring island's famous regatta week which attracted yachts from many distant sailing centres. Presumably in 1977 he had competed in *Thalia*.

'You can be skipper today, old chap. I'll be glad to relax and keep bar,' said Terence.

Raine had crewed for her brother before, and Jeff, too, had some experience. Between them they soon had *Mazinga* under way while the passengers sat in the bows or on the coach-roof.

No sooner were they out of harbour than, with almost no swell to speak of, Gloria began to feel seasick. Amy, who was sitting beside her when the girl turned pale and looked distressed, asked Terence if he had any anti-seasick pills on board.

'Seasick in this lovely weather? Oh, well, a tot of brandy will soon put her right,' was his reaction.

He disappeared below to fetch it and Sarah, aware of her ignorance of sailing but with a strong feeling that brandy was not the right curative, moved aft to speak quietly to Lyle.

'Gloria's feeling queasy. What's the best thing to do for her?'

He expressed no surprise. 'I'll come and have a look at her.'

Sarah stayed in the background, but near enough to hear

him say kindly, 'I'm sorry you're not feeling well, Gloria. Did you have any breakfast this morning?'

She shook her head. She was a plump girl who probably skipped breakfast in the hope of losing weight.

'Then that's half your trouble,' said Lyle. 'Eat some dry biscuits and you'll feel better. Biscuits or bread. Plenty of water. No alcohol,' were his succinct directions to Amy.

'Should I take her inside to lie down?'

'No, she wouldn't feel better below. She can lie down here on the coach-roof with some cushions to make it more comfortable.' As Terence returned with the brandy, he shook his head. 'Don't give her that. Have you any Stugeron tablets?'

Although he had ceded command of the expedition, the Irishman did not look pleased at having his advice countered. As the taller man went back to the cockpit, Terence said, 'I may as well drink it myself, then.' He swallowed the brandy at a gulp before fetching the remedies prescribed by Lyle.

Soon Gloria was feeling better, although not to the extent of enjoying the voyage as much as Sarah did.

For her, it was an experience akin to the Sunday afternoon when, invited by old Mr Morris, the antique dealer, to have tea with his invalid wife, she had walked into their sitting-room, filled with the treasures acquired during his many years in the trade, and thought—This is it. This is for me.

Now, as *Mazinga* skimmed over the ocean, powered by the wind instead of by a noisy, smelly engine, she thought again—This is it. I want this as part of my life.

She longed to have Lyle's expertise, and determined to learn how to sail so that, on another occasion, she could crew as usefully as Raine.

It would have been a perfect day—if there had been only the three of them, Lyle, Raine and herself, and if he had been less unfriendly. She felt she was the only one there who received no share of his attention. From Jeff, Cleve and Dudley it was difficult to detach herself, but at no time during the picnic did Lyle sit with her, or swim with her.

The wayzgoose ended with an impromptu party in the newspaper building where, with the hearty appetites induced by a long day on and in the water, they feasted on meat patties and cheeseburgers from a café which was open on Sunday evening.

This time it was Dudley who walked Sarah home. Before his arrival the paper had depended on the services of his father, the town's commercial photographer, who was better at portraiture than at news photography.

Although he was less well known to the general public, Dudley's reputation as a news photographer was as high as Lyle's as a reporter. Equally sated with strife and disaster, he had wanted to return to his birthplace, but not if there was no other scope for his talents than following in his father's footsteps. The reason he had not been on the staff from the outset was that he had been working out a contract with a French weekly news magazine.

'Where would you advise me to take sailing lessons, Dudley?' she asked, as they walked home together. His parents lived in the same road as the Charbonnes. 'Would the water sports instructor at the Paradise Reef Hotel take a non-resident, do you suppose?'

'Very likely—for a fat fee. Why waste your money when there are plenty of people who'd be glad to teach you for nothing? Me, for instance.'

'It's very kind of you to suggest it, but I want to take an intensive course. I couldn't expect you to coach me on that basis.'

'Why not? It takes about twelve hours' tuition to make a competent helmsman—I'm talking about small boat sailing—with individual instruction. Plus some homework from sailing manuals. If you want to find out if I'm competent to teach you, check me out at the Yacht Club. I've been sailing since I was seven when my father bought be a Cadet which I had until I was sixteen. If you like, and we're both of us free tomorrow about four o'clock, I'll give you a trial lesson in my father's old *Wayfarer*.'

They had reached her gate by this time. Sarah hesitated before replying. If she accepted his offer, would it lead to complications? She could tell that he found her attractive, and she liked him, in a friendly way.

He was of medium height, with a slight but well-knit figure and, like Lyle's secretary, a hint of Chinese blood in the shape of his features, although his skin was much darker than Vashti's.

'All right—thank you. See you tomorrow. Goodnight,' she said, with a smile.

'Goodnight.' He gave her his pleasant grin and went on his way.

The next morning Raine rushed into the office.

'It's hail and farewell, I'm afraid. I've got to fly home post-haste.'

'Oh, Raine—why?' Sarah exclaimed.

'While we were all basking yesterday, my poor mother-in-law slipped on an icy sidewalk and broke her wrist. Paul telephoned me before breakfast. It's a shame I have to go back so much sooner than I planned, but it can't be helped. We'll come down together next time, and bring the babies. Goodbye, Sarah dear.'

Raine bent and kissed her on both cheeks before saying goodbye to the others.

Her sailing lesson later that day was one of the most pleasant hours Sarah had ever spent. The *Wayfarer* was a sturdy Bermudan rig dinghy which could be raced by a helmsman and crew, and cruised by a family of four.

Having given her a buoyancy waistcoat like the one he was wearing, Dudley talked to her briefly about safety, and then took her out on a quiet reach of the large harbour to demonstrate the three basics of sailing—reaching, running and beating. Before the lesson was over, he had also shown her tacking and gybing, and what was meant by sitting out, luffing and easing the mainsheet.

A patient and lucid teacher, he stressed the importance of never having the mainsheet made fast when sailing a small boat, and the need to let go all sheets when in trouble. Sarah could only have enjoyed the time more had Lyle been her instructor, and perhaps she would not have learnt as much. It was easier to concentrate with a teacher who might have a disturbing effect on other girls, but not on her.

After the lesson he took her to his parents' house where his mother made coffee for them while Dudley demonstrated a few useful knots. Finding that Sarah, like himself, was an early riser, he suggested a second lesson before breakfast the following day.

It did not take long for the purchase of her little house to be completed. Complicated searches, and the delays caused by the vendor's and buyer's solicitors being in different towns, did not arise in this instance. Very soon Sarah was the excited owner of Cordia Cottage, as she intended to call it, taking the name from the tree in the garden.

She decided to move in at once, putting up with the inconvenience of having it done up while she was living there for the pleasure of being in her own place.

As a parting gift to the Charbonnes, to whom she was grateful for their kindness, she bought them a cut glass vase which she knew Susan admired.

She was soon on terms with her neighbours who, like most of the people in that area, were hard-up but respectable artisans. On one side lived a joiner and his family; on the other a retired roadmender whose wife still worked as a seamstress.

A month passed without event. She and Dudley fell into the habit of sailing together most mornings between sunrise and breakfast. This they had in a waterfront café, changing their clothes at the office.

In the evenings, and at weekends, she no longer went to Emerald Hill, being too busy with her own small property.

Her contact with Lyle was as much and no more than it would have been had there been nothing between them but their professional association. Occasionally he would have a brief conversation about something unconnected with their work, as when he told her that, since buying the antique sideboard from old Mrs Rudolph, he had been offered other pieces of furniture by people in the same village.

Spending much of her free time painting the cottage, inside and out, Sarah also spent many hours pondering the enigma of his coolness towards her.

Once she wrote a long letter to Liz, telling her everything—but glossing over the details of the episode in his car—and asking her opinion and advice. But the letter was never posted. The next morning she tore it up. Her feelings about Lyle were too private to be shared with anyone, even her oldest and closest friend.

All the heart-searching ever suffered by a girl in love was suffered by Sarah in that period when he was so strangely cool towards her. Over and over again, she recapitulated all she had ever said to him or he to her.

But the only reason I'm a virgin is because I never met anyone I felt sure would make the first time wonderful for me. You could do that, couldn't you, Lyle?

Had she made the fatal mistake of forgetting that man is a hunter? Had it been that ingenuous invitation which had put him off her?

His immediate reaction hadn't been cool—anything but!

But afterwards he had called her Delilah, and earlier the same day he had said—*I wasn't planning to do that, but you have an unfortunate knack of oversetting my good intentions.*

One evening the joiner next door screwed to her gate a

nameplate, *Cordia Cottage*, which he had had made on her behalf. The next night both sets of neighbours came in for refreshments, and to see how her house was arranged. Her curtains and the cover for the studio couch had been made for her by Mrs Jackson, the seamstress.

As yet, no one at the paper knew that she was ready for guests, and the dinner *à deux*, which Lyle had said he would hold her to, now seemed an impossibility.

The next afternoon, Sarah answered the internal telephone and heard Gloria say, 'Front office. There's a gentleman to see you, Miss Graham—A Mr Benson.'

'I'll be right down, Gloria.'

Preoccupied with the women's page story she was writing, she picked up her notebook and pencil and ran down the two flights of stairs, hoping the interruption would not take long.

Like most newspapers, the *Independent* had already attracted one or two cranks who, on various pretexts, came in to talk to the reporters. Such people were quickly recognised as time-wasters, but, unless everyone was exceptionally busy, usually someone would go down and listen patiently to them. On the other hand, Mr Benson might be the bearer of useful information.

There were only two people in the front office when she pushed open the inner door. One was a woman filling in an advertisement form, and the other was Mr Benson. At the sight of him, Sarah gave an exclamation of disbelief.

'*Roddy!* W-what are you doing here?'

'Visiting you. How are you, Sarah?'

Before she had recovered from her astonishment, he stepped closer and hugged her.

When he drew back, Sarah had quickly to school her expression to hide the acute dismay which followed hard on her amazement. The last person she wanted to see at this difficult juncture of her life was Roderick Benson. It showed how little thought she had given to him since leaving England that the name Benson hadn't reminded her of him.

'Why didn't you let me know you were coming?' she asked.

'It was a spur-of-the-moment decision. We can't talk here. Is there a coffee shop or a bar we can go to?'

'I can't leave the office until one of the others comes back. Someone has to be always on call in case a big news story breaks. You'd better come up to the reporters' room for a few minutes.'

She knew she didn't sound very welcoming, but how could she when his out-of-the-blue arrival, and its implications, filled her with apprehension?

'How long are you here for? Where are you staying?' she asked, as she led the way upstairs.

'At the moment the answer to both those questions is: I don't know. I came on a stand-by flight. Someone had to cancel at the last moment, and I took their place. As for where I'll be staying, I shan't know that until I call at the Tourist Office. The Tourist Information desk at the airport rang through to their main office to ask them to locate a room for me. I stipulated a good hotel. I don't want to be stuck in a cheap one, or a guesthouse,' said Roddy grandly.

'You may have no choice. It's high season, and most of the hotels are fully booked. Oh, Roddy, what an impetuous thing to do! My life is so full at the moment that I've hardly any time to spare.'

'What does that mean? That you've got a romance on the go? Your mother implied as much the last time she talked to mine.'

'Your mother must have misunderstood her. It's not romance which occupies my time. It's work, and learning to sail, and——' Sarah bit off the rest. If he hadn't already heard about it via their mothers, she didn't want Roddy to know about her little house.

'You can ring up the Tourist Office from here,' she said, as they reached the second floor. 'If they've found somewhere for you to stay, as soon as I'm free I'll run you up there. I've bought a small car. It's impossible to manage without one here. There are buses to most parts of the island, but the timetables are geared to workers and at other times the services aren't frequent.'

While she was speaking, she found and dialled the number for him.

Roddy took the receiver from her and, after a short conversation, put his hand over the mouthpiece and asked, 'What sort of place is the Paradise Reef Hotel?'

'The most expensive on the island.'

Without asking her how expensive, Roddy told the person on the line that he would accept a room at the Paradise Reef. Before he had finished the call Jimmy came in, and Sarah was able to leave him on telephone duty while she attended to her unexpected and unwelcome visitor.

'You're not too busy to dine with me tonight, I hope?' he said, as they set out for the southern side of the island.

'No, I'm not working this evening, but I shall be tomorrow night, and it's my weekend on duty.'

'Won't one of the others stand in for you if you explain the situation?'

'I don't like to ask that sort of favour, Roddy. It's not as if we've all been working together for a long time. A girl has to be doubly careful not to seem to impose on her colleagues. You still haven't told me how long you're staying.'

'It depends. I'm hoping for a stand-by flight back, but I haven't been into that yet.'

Sarah did not ask what it depended on. To keep the conversation as impersonal as possible, she began to point out features of the landscape, including the ancient pain tree.

'Why is it called that?' he asked.

'Because the leaves were brewed, or used as a poultice, to cure almost every known ailment. The tree had to be rewarded with a penny, or a nail hammered into the bark. Did you know there were once camels here? They were brought in to carry the cane.'

She went on talking about Compostela, its turbulent past and hopeful future, until they arrived at the hotel. There they had a swim and a drink, and then Sarah drove back to town to change for her dinner date with him.

At the Paradise Reef, in the season, men were expected to wear ties if not coats, and women to put on evening dresses. The only dress in her wardrobe which was suitable for the hotel was one she had bought to have ready for a special occasion. But tonight was not the occasion she had had in mind. She had hoped that Lyle would be the first man for whom she would wear the drifting folds of honey-coloured cotton voile scattered with black flowers and leaves.

Roddy was waiting for her in the bar when she returned. He was wearing a white dinner jacket which made her bite her lip in mingled amusement and embarrassment. How typical of him! Far from looking distinguished and rich which, presumably, was the intended effect, he reminded her of the people in films revived from her parents' youth.

His face lit up when he saw her pausing in the entrance. He slid off his stool and came to meet her. 'You look wonderful, Sarah.'

She smiled and said, 'Thank you,' but his admiration gave her no pleasure. There was only one man in the world she wanted to look at her like that.

At the bar Roddy argued with her when she asked for a fruit drink, but Sarah was not to be budged from her no-alcohol-when-driving rule.

'I think we should dine soon. You'll be feeling tired early tonight. Everyone does for the first few days,' she told him, remembering her own arrival.

Roddy didn't like the table they were given, close to the service doors. Instead of quietly requesting a more secluded one, he made a fuss. Inwardly, she cringed. She was thankful there were not many people there, except the staff who were too well trained to show their feelings. Perhaps they were used to brash behaviour.

Near the second table to which they were shown was one for a party of twelve. Later that night a combo would play for dancing, but Sarah hoped to be gone before them.

Roddy studied the menu and, predictably, chose all the most expensive dishes. Again Sarah had to be firm to withstand being coerced into eating more than she wanted. What an effort it was to be with him, she thought. The antithesis of being with Lyle, with whom—were it not for her emotional involvement—she would never feel any friction.

Lyle in an old pair of shorts had more presence, more natural authority, than Roddy in his silk tweed dinner jacket, with his gold watch and Gucci shoes, and all the other fashionable status symbols that bolstered his uncertain self-confidence.

As the thought of Lyle slipped into her mind, the man himself entered the restaurant. He was bringing up the rear of a large group of people but, being so tall, was immediately visible above their heads.

Apart from him, there were only three others Sarah recognised, the Deputy Premier and his wife, and their grown-up daughter. The other eight people were strangers to her. Four of them were Compostelans, and four were recently arrived Europeans, their midwinter pallor a marked contrast to the dark skins of their companions.

'Who are this lot, I wonder?' asked Roddy.

'The thick-set man with the glasses is the Deputy Premier.'

'I recognise the tall fellow. It's Lyle Talbot, the TV reporter,' said Roddy. 'I suppose he's on holiday here.'

Sarah was surprised that her mother had been able to resist telling Mrs Benson who her daughter was working for. Perhaps that was her father's doing. Sarah had told him that Lyle wanted to play down his fame as a television person. If Roddy didn't know what Lyle was doing in Compostela, she saw no reason to mention it unless she was obliged to.

Would Lyle spot her?

She was seated with her back to the large table, wearing a dress he had never seen, and dining with a young man he didn't know. There was a chance he wouldn't notice her and, even if he did, he might not feel obliged to come over and say hello.

But if he did see her, and felt no curiosity about Roddy, it would suggest that, although on three occasions he had kissed her, since then something had happened to make him lose interest in her.

An unpleasant thought occurred to her. Lyle's coolness stemmed from the day, during his sister's visit, when he had had lunch with the Deputy Premier. Sarah had assumed that it had been an all-male working lunch. But perhaps it had been a more social occasion attended by the Minister's wife and daughter.

The girl was clever, an Oxford graduate whom Sarah had interviewed for the women's page on her recent return from England. She was not particularly attractive, being thick-legged and lumpy-hipped. But she had a pleasant personality, and from now on she meant to devote herself to improving the lot of women in Compostela.

Could it be that Lyle saw in her a means of cementing his position among the island's most influential people?

The party at present in power was likely to stay there. The only other major political force was Communist-dominated, and in the foreseeable future the Compostelans were unlikely to vote for extremists.

They had, in their time, endured a poverty as severe if not worse than the hardship which had made Cuba ripe for a Communist take-over. But poor as they had been in the past and, in many cases, still were, Sarah could not see the Compostelans with their unquenchable humour and their love of colour and music submitting to a régime which, so Dudley had told her, made all women equal by rationing their clothes. In Cuba, no one was allowed to have more than one pair of good shoes a year, one pair of everyday shoes, one blouse, one skirt, and one metre of good material or one and a half metres of basic material.

The very idea of such restrictions would raise an outcry among the Compostelan seamstresses and their customers. Nor was it at all probable that Compostelan men would submit to regular assessments of their performances by their fellow workers, as was now the case in Cuba. According to Dudley even to say *Adiós*, or *Jesús!* when someone sneezed was no longer acceptable, and *Señor* and *Señora* had been replaced by *Compañero* and *Compañera*, meaning Comrade.

But that would not happen in Compostela where a peaceful and less drastic revolution was in progress. The Minister's post was secure and, as his son-in-law, Lyle would no longer be subject to disapproval by certain members of the Government who would have preferred to see the *Independent* run by a Compostelan.

Sick at heart at the thought that this might explain his failure to follow up his embrace in the car, she dropped her napkin and was bending to retrieve it when the rearguard of the Minister's party passed by.

Would his wife dispose their guests so that Lyle and her daughter were seated next to each other? Sarah dared not turn round to find out.

CHAPTER EIGHT

THE rest of the meal tasted like ashes in her mouth. Now she was torn between hoping that Roddy would soon become sleepy, and wanting to stay and observe Lyle's attitude to the Minister's daughter. But not to be observed herself.

Enquiries about Roddy's sisters and mutual friends kept the conversation going until the coffee stage. She wanted to keep him talking on harmless subjects. If she gave him half a chance he might launch on another declaration, and that would be the last straw.

Considering how firmly she had turned him down, the day before signing her contract with Lyle, she thought it amazingly importunate of him to pursue her to the Caribbean.

The combo arrived: a pianist, a clarinettist and a bass-player. They played on the terrace outside the restaurant, so the music was not so loud as to make conversation difficult.

'Shall we dance?' Roddy asked, when the combo began their second number.

'Let's wait. I don't like being first on the floor.'

'We shan't be. Those people will,' he said, indicating a couple who had started dinner before them, and were now on their way to the floor.

'Come on.' He rose and reached for her hand, making it impossible to refuse.

Sarah did not look at the table for twelve as she passed it, hand in hand with Roddy. He danced as well as he played tennis, and there had been a time when she had enjoyed dancing with him and had let herself go as uninhibitedly as he did. But not tonight. Nothing could impair her natural sense of rhythm, but tonight her movements were restrained by selfconsciousness.

The fast number which had enabled Roddy to show off his agility and perfect tempo was succeeded by a slow, romantic number. For this, although the floor was not crowded, he put both arms round her and changed to a night-club shuffle.

As they revolved, Sarah snatched covert glances at the table for twelve. The Minister's daughter was dancing with one of her father's European guests. The chair beside Lyle's was empty, and he was talking across the table to one of the Compostelans. But who had been sitting next to him was still in question because half the party was dancing.

'Let's take a break, Roddy,' she said, after the second dance.

He looked surprised—they had often danced for an hour without tiring—but agreed. Sarah walked off the floor, her head turned away from the Minister's table.

Scarcely had she sat down when Lyle's voice said smoothly, 'Good evening, Sarah.'

Roddy, caught in the act of sitting down, straightened again. Reluctantly, Sarah raised her eyes to Lyle's face.

'Good evening. This is Roderick Benson ... Lyle Talbot.'

'You don't need an introduction, Mr Talbot,' said Roddy, as they shook hands. 'Sarah didn't tell me she'd met you. Interviewed you for her paper, I suppose?'

'No, I interviewed her,' Lyle said dryly. When Roddy looked puzzled, he added, 'She works for me. I own the paper.'

Roddy's puzzlement changed to astonishment. 'You didn't tell me that, Sarah.'

'She's a surprising girl, as you may find out when you've known her longer,' was Lyle's comment.

'I've already known her a long time,' said Roddy. 'How long?'—looking at her. 'Eight years?'

It was Lyle's turn to look surprised.

'About that,' she agreed. 'Roddy's parents are friends of my parents.'

'And you're also working in Compostela, Benson? What a happy coincidence,' said Lyle. 'Another of Sarah's surprises, and one which explains a great deal.'

What did he mean by that remark?

'No, no—I'm not working here. I just flew over to see her,' Roddy explained.

'Indeed?' Lyle's dark eyes appraised the younger man's appearance. He himself was conforming to the hotel's after-dark rule by wearing a very lightweight suit with a Polynesian-print shirt and a plain tie. 'How long are you here for?'

'A week at least. Perhaps longer.'

'As you've come such a long way to see her, we must try to arrange for her to have extra time off. We'll talk about it in the morning, Sarah. Meanwhile, enjoy yourselves.'

With a bow, he returned to his table.

'He seems a nice chap,' said Roddy, resuming his seat. 'Why didn't you tell me you worked for him?'

'I—I wasn't too pleased to see him here. It's . . . inhibiting, in one's time off, to be under surveillance by one's boss.'

'Then we'll go somewhere else.' Roddy signalled to their waiter.

'You should go to bed,' said Sarah. 'Aren't you tired?'

He asked for the bill. 'Not a bit. Probably the fact that I never do go to bed early has something to do with it.'

'But, Roddy, by your body's time-clock it's after two in the morning! I'm sure you'll flake out before long.'

'In a couple of hours from now, maybe. Not yet. We'll go back to the bar,' he decided, signing the bill and adding his room number.

'I suppose if I ask you back to my room, you'll say no?' he added, as they left the restaurant. 'It would be entirely respectable. I've a sitting-room as well as a bedroom, and a fridge with some complimentary drinks in it. We can relax properly there. You can kick off your shoes if you want to.'

'I don't want to,' Sarah replied. 'To be honest, I want to go home. I *am* tired, and now my head aches. I'm sorry, Roddy, but you'll have to excuse me tonight.'

At once he became all concern, offering to drive her home and return to the hotel by taxi.

By the time she had dissuaded him, said goodnight, and driven away, her temples were throbbing with pain. She had had as much tension as she could take, and wanted nothing but to crawl into bed and blot the whole miserable evening out of her mind.

Within an hour of Lyle's arrival at the office the next day, Vashti came to tell Sarah that he wished to see her. She had checked the diary before he arrived.

When she entered his room, he said, 'Good morning. I've been looking at the diary to see what adjustments can be made so that your young man doesn't find himself at too much of a loose end. For a start, you can have this weekend off.'

She said stiffly, 'It's good of you to be so concerned, but Roddy is not my young man, and I shouldn't dream of foisting my weekend duty on to one of the others.'

Lyle rose and walked round his desk to close the door on to the landing. The inner door of his office led through to a room known as the Morgue. There, in several large filing cabinets, they were beginning to build up comprehensive files on all aspects of island life. The room took its name from the cabinet which housed the files on local people, particularly the notabilities whose lives would one day be worthy of a detailed obituary notice.

Lyle said, 'Commendable scruples—but unnecessary. I shall take over the weekend duty, at no inconvenience since I shall be working in any case.' He paused. 'Perhaps it would have been more accurate to refer to Benson as *one* of your young men—although he must think he can claim a certain priority. No one flies across the Atlantic to see a girl who means little to them.'

'He flew on stand-by, which is cheaper.'

'But still expensive,' he said dryly.

'If you must know, he asked me to marry him, just before I left England. I told him I didn't love him, but Roddy isn't accustomed to not having whatever he wants. His family are wealthy, and he spends money like water. Flying here doesn't mean to him as much as it would to most people.'

Lyle looked thoughtfully at her for some moments. 'You didn't appear to be discouraging his suit last night.'

'I could hardly refuse to have dinner with him. He is still a friend,' she retorted.

'For whom you put on a dress which, according to the women at my table, was one for a special occasion. In fact it was the consensus of opinion that it wouldn't be long before I had to replace you.'

'I chose the dress to suit the place. Your friends were jumping to conclusions—as I might have jumped to the conclusion that you had your eye on the D.P.M.'s daughter.'

His dark eyes narrowed. 'Did you think that?'

She shrugged. 'It would be a very advantageous marriage.'

'As would yours to Benson if money is no object with him.'

'I could never marry for money.'

'But you're quick to ascribe venal motives to others.'

'I didn't say I thought you *were* chasing her; only that it was a possibility as feasible as what your friends thought about me and Roddy.'

'They were not my friends,' he corrected her. 'The editor of a paper has to have contacts in all quarters if he's to do his job properly. The D.P.M. is, I think, an honest politician who wants what's best for the island as much as power for himself. They were all pleasant, decent people with whom I have little in common except a desire to preserve this corner of the Caribbean from *all* forms of exploitation, including the Marxist-Leninist variety. My friends are nearly all journalists, one of them being my brother-in-law.'

He turned back to his desk, and picked up a package.

'I heard from my sister yesterday. She sent me some things I wanted, and this for you.'

'I—I wonder what it can be?' said Sarah.

'Why not open it and see?' For the first time in a long time there was a hint of warmth in his eyes.

There were two layers of wrapping; deep violet paper over paler violet tissue. They enclosed what at first she took to be a vivid pink scarf or stole until, shaken out, the silk resolved itself into a pair of the narrow oriental trousers which Raine had worn.

Sarah's face lit up.

'Churidars! And in my favourite colour. How good of her!'

'There's a message with them.' Lyle bent to pick up a piece of cardboard which had slipped to the floor.

On one side was printed *With Love*. On the other Raine had written—*For the delectation of the man in your life*.

Had his sister guessed who the man was? The trousers would be perfect for a dinner *à deux* at Cordia Cottage, if she had the courage to invite him. The words trembled on her tongue, but were never uttered because before she could say them there was a knock on the door.

'Come in.'

Jimmy looked in. 'Telephone, Sarah.'

'Just coming.'

Lyle said, 'If it's Benson on the line for you, remember you'll be free all weekend.'

'But I——'

Don't argue. Off you go.' Already he was back at his desk, beginning to sub someone's copy.

Roddy stayed for a week. He had to. Having, on Sunday, repeated his proposal, and once again been turned down, he had to wait four more days before he could get on a flight to London.

Before they parted, he said wryly, 'It's a great life you have here, Sarah. I don't think you'll ever come back. I'm not sure I should, in your place.'

She watched the plane take off, and was relieved to be free of the obligation to spend time with him.

It was as he had said. She had a new life. Lyle, sailing, her job, the cottage, the colourful beauty of the island supplied all her needs. The weekly letter from her parents, and less frequent bulletins from Liz, were links she would not want to break. But they never made her feel homesick. How could they? She was at home here, more at home than ever before.

Where Lyle was concerned, she felt that whatever had caused the very marked coolness in his manner no longer obtained. All the same, she didn't intend inviting him to the cottage a second time. He had said he would take her up on her first invitation, and he wasn't the kind of man who forgot things like that—unless it suited him.

On the second Sunday after Roddy's departure, Terence invited Sarah, with Dudley and Jeff, to spend the day sailing *Mazinga*.

However, when she arrived the other two were not there.

'Dudley's had a tip that someone extremely famous flew in incognito yesterday,' Terence explained. 'He's determined to check it out, so he and Jeff will join us later. I've told them where we'll be at lunch-time, and they'll drive over and join us there. Dudley says you're a competent crew now, so between us we should be able to sail her as far as Shell Creek, wouldn't you say?'

'No problem,' Sarah agreed.

She was looking forward to applying her new skills on board *Mazinga*.

To reach Shell Creek, they had to pass Emerald Hill. There was no one on either of the beaches, nor could she see any figures on the terrace or the balcony above it. But if Lyle was in his room and, recognising *Mazinga* by her distinctive orange spinnaker, used a pair of fieldglasses to see who was on board her, he might wonder what she was doing alone with his advertisement manager.

It took them under two hours to arrive at Shell Creek where they swam, and chatted, and waited for the others to turn up. There were several other yachts at anchor, and three or four picnic parties on the beach. But Compostela had so many beautiful beaches that none was ever over-crowded, even on Sundays.

Terence was a pleasant companion and Sarah couldn't help wondering why, by this time, he hadn't acquired a girl-friend. It was not for lack of interest in women; she had seen the way he eyed pretty faces and shapely figures, although his manner towards her had never been even mildly amorous.

'It looks as if there's been some hold-up. I think we should start lunch without them,' he said when, at half past one, there was still no sign of the others.

They had lunch on deck, under the awning: chicken roti with salad and white wine.

'You and Dudley seem to spend a lot of time together. Is there romance in the air?' Terence asked her, while they were eating.

'Heavens, no! Only friendship,' said Sarah. 'We sail together most mornings, but that's all. We don't spend any other time together.'

'So you're like me, eh? Fancy-free?'

She made a non-committal sound. Yes was untrue, but to say No would invite questions.

'Did Dudley have any idea who this famous person might be? What exactly did he say?' she asked.

'Not much. He was in a tearing hurry to get on the trail. It could be that it's turned out to be a bigger story than he anticipated, and he and Jeff have gone back to the office to print the pictures and write it up straight away. It may even be a major scoop. Anyway, if they don't turn up at all, I'm quite happy with my present company.'

He tacked on this last remark in the manner of a man being gallant for politeness' sake rather than from sincerity.

After lunch, when Sarah said she would like to do some shelling, he said, 'By all means. You won't mind if I don't join you, I hope. A snooze is more in my line on Sunday afternoon.'

Leaving him stretched in the sun, she went ashore by herself and spent an hour hunting for shells and chatting to other people similarly engaged.

Terence was asleep when she rowed the dinghy back to *Mazinga* and climbed on board. She went below and washed up their few lunch things. Then she made a pot of tea, found some biscuits, and carried the tea tray on deck.

Before she woke him, she looked down at his sleeping face, thinking that, unlike Lyle, Terence would not be a good subject for a sculptor. His hair grew low on his forehead and he had a small, unmanly nose, and too small a mouth. His bright blue eyes and his personality gave him a certain charm when he was awake. But asleep there was nothing about him to arrest the eye as there was with Lyle.

She wondered if there would ever be a morning when she would open her eyes and find Lyle's head on the next pillow, or her cheek pillowed on his strong shoulder.

Presently, drinking tea, she said, 'If we start back now, there'll be time to put in at Emerald Hill and find out what's been going on. If they have got a scoop, the others are sure to have been in touch with Lyle.'

And I can make it clear to him that I'm not alone with Terence by choice, and perhaps I can stay ashore and spend the evening there, she thought.

There was no reason why Terence should not sail *Mazinga* singlehanded. She was only a thirty-foot sloop, and her winches made her very easy to handle, except perhaps in a squall.

He received this suggestion without enthusiasm.

'Yes, we could, I suppose. Actually I was planning to have another swim in that bay we passed on the way here, about half a mile east of Emerald Hill.' He checked the time by his watch. 'There's time to do both.'

Possibly, not being a journalist, he was not as eager as she was to hear the outcome of the others' investigations. Certainly Emerald Hill held no special attraction for him.

They anchored well out in the bay which he wanted to explore, and rowed to the beach over shallowly submerged stretches of reef and several huge growths of brain coral.

'This is a wonderful snorkelling ground, yet there's nobody here,' Sarah remarked. 'The beach must be difficult to get to by land.'

'Yes, it seems exclusive to the goats,' said Terence, pointing out a few animals at one end of the strand.

They swam, then returned to the sloop and secured the dinghy astern. Sarah was blotting herself dry, preparatory to going below to change her bikini for a tee-shirt and shorts, when Terence took her by surprise. One moment she was patting herself with the towel and looking forward to their next stop at Emerald Hill. The next, she was in his arms.

'Terence!' she exclaimed in protest, when, having kissed her, he drew his head back to look at her.

'You can do better than that, baby. Come on now, give,' he said hoarsely.

His next kiss was like a remora attaching itself to her unwilling mouth. She attempted to push him away, which made his arms tighten around her. He was trying to force open her lips, and she could tell he was very excited. She began to struggle more violently.

The ensuing tussle frightened her. He was neither a tall nor a strong man, but he was a man, and therefore stronger than herself, particularly when he was actuated by this sudden upsurge of lust. Instinctively, Sarah realised that he was ignoring her resistance because he was in the grip of a hunger too long repressed and now wholly out of control.

When at last she broke free, she was trembling with shock and disgust. Terence was between her and the hatch, or she would have taken refuge below, shot the bolts and stayed there until he cooled down. As it was, she could only back away from him.

'Don't, Terence ... p-please ... you've n-no right ...' was her stammered appeal.

'Come on, now. I'm not going to hurt you. There's no need to fight me.' His tone was wheedling, but his eyes weren't. They were bloodshot, and horribly determined. 'Don't tell me you've never been ******' He used a term which made her flinch.

Her panic gave place to anger. 'No, I haven't—and even if I had, I wouldn't let you touch me.'

The unwisdom of speaking the truth was made clear by the glare in his eyes. 'You'll be sorry you said that,' he snarled. 'I've already had my face slapped by that stuck-up little half-breed bitch. I'm not going to take any high-hat nonsense from you!'

She knew then that what she had been unwilling to believe on the night he had walked her home was true. Terence was a racialist.

Anyone who could refer to the lovely, sweet-natured Vashti in those contemptuous terms must be ridden with racism. If Vashti was 'a half-breed bitch' to him, what was his private opinion of the most African-looking of the Compostelans?

To Sarah, her father's daughter, the face of race-hatred was as loathsome as the danger of being raped. Even then, with his lecherous gaze stripping her naked, she wasn't sure he would go as far as to rape her. He might come to his senses before that. But it wasn't a chance she was going to take.

The usual method of entering the water from the deck—other than by going down the boarding ladder—was to climb outside the pulpit or over the wire lifelines, and poise there briefly before diving. But if she did that, he would grab her.

She ran at the rails and vaulted, her hand barely touching the stanchion as her slim figure sprang into space, then plummeted into the water. As soon as she surfaced, she struck out, hearing furious shouts from above her. But, not being much of a swimmer, Terence wasn't likely to dive in after her, and by the time he had brought the dinghy round to the ladder, she would have a good start. He could only row in pursuit. He did have a small outboard motor to power the dinghy, but it wasn't on board at the moment. It was at the boatyard, having a wash out and fresh plugs.

Having swum hard for a hundred yards, Sarah rolled face-up and, still swimming, looked back to see what he was doing. To her relief he was still on deck, yelling and waving his arms like a man demented.

When Sarah waded ashore, she was panting from exertion, but the weakness she felt in her legs was reaction after a nasty scare.

Terence was no longer visible. Perhaps he had gone below to have a stiff drink. He was probably as scared as she had been; scared of the accusations she might make against him.

By now the goats had disappeared, but their droppings marked the track they had taken. There seemed to be a network of trails through the thorny scrub of the hinter-land. As it was getting late in the day, she hoped that they might be wending their way to a village. She wished she knew more of their habits. All over the island, unattended small herds were to be seen foraging the roadsides.

But how their owners distinguished them from other herds, or knew where to find them, or whether the goats provided milk as well as meat, she had no idea.

Above goat-height, in places the track was blocked by prickly branches which she had to disentangle before she could make her way past. It wasn't long before her limbs and almost unprotected body bore many scratches, some deep enough to trickle blood. Her feet suffered most. The track was rough and stony, and her heels and soles, regu-larly creamed now that they were always on display, were even softer than they had been in England.

Twice she thought she was going round in circles and would find herself back at the beach before she found her way out. But at last the track came to a bank at the top of which was a tarred road with two cars disappearing along it.

They were the last cars to pass. Sarah saw none as she walked an uncomfortable mile on sun-baked macadam to the junction with the Emerald Hill dirt road.

In a way she was glad no more came by. It would have been difficult to explain why, clad in nothing but a bikini, with dirty, sore feet and thorn-pricked from shoulder to ankle, she was trudging along on her own. On a day, moreover, when most of the islanders, if not at the beach, were dressed in their best.

Soon after turning in at the mouth of the dirt road, she heard a car slowing on the main road. She stopped and looked over her shoulder, and recognised Lyle's car. He was alone.

Straightening her drooping shoulders, she pinned on a smile. In the manner of someone nearing the end of a pleasant country ramble, she waved to him as he drove closer.

Lyle stopped the car alongside her, taking in her sweat-shiny face, the dust on her legs, the scratches.

'What the devil have you been doing with yourself?'

'I've been playing Cowboys and Indians,' she said, with attempted flippancy. Then her lips quivered, and she added, 'I'm very tired, Lyle. Don't ask questions. Just take me up to the house and give me a cold drink, would you?'

He must have seen her mouth tremble, and heard the strain in her voice. He pushed open the passenger door, and Sarah climbed in and sank back with a sigh of relief that she didn't have to walk any further.

At the entrance to his drive, he said quietly, 'Tell me one thing. Has anything happened that the police ought to know about?'

'No . . . no, nothing like that.' She mustn't dissolve into tears. Not now; when it was all over, except for the explanation. 'You haven't a handkerchief I could borrow, have you?'

Lyle opened the glove box and gave her a packet of tissues. By the time they drew up at the house, she was in control of herself again. Not completely, but well enough.

Striving neither to wince nor to hobble, she stepped out of the car and began to walk to the verandah. She had taken only a few steps when he came round from his side of the car and picked her up.

'How far did you walk with bare feet?'

'I—I'm not sure. Maybe a mile.'

The front door was closed, suggesting the house was empty.

Lyle said, 'The key's in my back pocket. Can you reach it?'

She slid her arm under his and felt for the pocket and, in it, the old-fashioned key. The keyhole was high in the door, easy for her to reach from her position in his arms. With the

door unlocked, he shouldered it open and carried her into
the hall and up the wide staircase.

'No one else is in at the moment, but they may come
back any time. I imagine you'd rather not see them until
you're cleaned up. We can handle that in my room.'

His bedroom had altered since the last time she had seen
it. There were proper bookshelves against the whole of one
wall, and a desk, and a large elbow chair in the manner of
Chippendale.

Lyle lowered her into it. Then he crouched to examine
her soles, the twist of his mouth suggesting they were not a
pleasant sight.

There was a vacuum jug on the desk, on a tray with an
upturned tumbler. He filled the tumbler from the jug and
handed it to her. Then he moved away to a cupboard,
returning a few moments later with some amber liquid in a
smaller glass.

'A brandy chaser before you have a warm shower. Then
I'll bathe your feet and patch them up. I'm going downstairs to the kitchen to fetch a bowl and the first aid box. I
shan't be long.'

While he was gone Sarah finished the water and sipped
the brandy, concerned about what she should tell him. The
truth would make him so angry he would fire Terence on
the spot. And Terence was good at his job. Where would
Lyle find as good a replacement for the paper's crucial first
months?

Before she had reached any conclusion, he came back
carrying a large plastic bowl and a metal case which looked
like a toolbox but was full of medical equipment.

After another brief absence in his bathroom, he reappeared.

'I've adjusted the thermostat for you. There's a clean
bath sheet on the rail, and a bottle of shampoo on the soap
tray if you want to wash your hair. Have a good sluice
down, but leave your feet to me.'

For the second time he scooped her up and carried her to the adjoining room.

Setting her down on the bathmat outside the shower, he said, 'Don't worry about getting blood on the towel. Call me when you're ready.'

The suds which streamed down her body when she rinsed the shampoo out of her hair smarted on the deepest scratches. But the warm water soothed and refreshed her. When she felt clean, she turned it off and towelled her hair until it stopped dripping down her neck. Then she dried her arms and her legs, and the tops of her toes and her insteps. Finally she wrapped the towel round her, kanga-fashion, and called out, 'I've finished, Lyle.'

This time he carried her to his bed, and laid her across it so that the light from the window would fall on her feet. He pushed pillows under her shoulders, making her comfortable.

'There's a lot of grit in the lacerations. Cleaning it out is going to hurt,' he warned her.

'Have you a bullet I can bite on?' she asked him, smiling.

What did it matter how much it hurt when he was being so kind and caring to her? Tender loving care from Lyle would make anything bearable.

He was as deft as a doctor, she thought, as he set to work. But before he was satisfied that all the abrasions were clean, she had had to clench her teeth hard to prevent any whimper escaping her.

'Good girl! You stood that very well. I'll put some temporary dressings on, and then I'll see to the scratches.'

For their treatment she had to sit up, on the edge of the bed, while he swabbed them with antiseptic. Having dealt with her shoulders and arms, he pushed the towel high up her thighs and swabbed the marks on her legs. Although he asked her no questions, she knew it could not be much longer before she had to account for the state she had been in half an hour ago.

'Your back next. You'll have to let the towel down.'

Obediently, Sarah shifted sideways, presenting her back to him. She let the towel slide to her hips, but kept her arms over her breasts.

Lyle sat behind her on the bed. 'Probably a swim would do these as much good as anything, but your feet are better kept dry. Are you much scratched at the front?'

'Not much. I can manage the front ones.'

'Don't worry. I wasn't planning to cover you with blushes as well as scratches,' was his sardonic comment. 'I concede the temptation, but feel I can manage to withstand it. I presume it was someone who couldn't who made you run off without shoes. Who was it? Dudley?'

The question was asked with a bite which betrayed his underlying anger.

'Dudley? No! He would never——' She stopped.

'Any man will overstep the mark if the provocation is strong enough. Dudley's obviously deeply enamoured, and——'

'That's nonsense,' she interrupted. 'We're sailing companions. There's never been anything else between us.'

'You surprise me. I would have said that it was between the sheets, not handling them, that Dudley saw you in his mind's eye.' He was making a caustic play on the yachtsman's term for the ropes used to trim a sail.

'If he did, he would have suggested that we spend other times together, apart from our early morning sailing. And today he's been chasing this scoop. Didn't he tell you?'

'What scoop? I know nothing about it.'

'He and Jeff were going to come sailing, but then someone told Dudley a VIP had arrived here, someone quite exceptionally newsworthy. I don't know any more than that, but——' She broke off at a hail from outside.

Lyle rose from the bed and opened the door to the balcony. He crossed to the balustrade and looked down at the terrace below. From where she was sitting, she could see him through the nearest window.

She heard him say, 'Oh, it's you, Terence. Is this a social call?'

Clutching the towel, Sarah moved quickly towards the doorway, biting her lips at the stabs of pain from her feet.

She was in time to hear Terence answer, 'No, it isn't. As a matter of fact I'm in a jam, and I need your advice. Something bloody awkward has happened.'

'What's the trouble?'

'Sarah asked me to take her sailing today. Like a fool—and I freely admit it—I let the minx lead me on. Damn me, I'd hardly laid a finger on her, when the silly kid panicked and jumped overboard. I did no more than kiss her, I swear it. But the way the girl swam ashore and hared off into the backwoods, you'd think I'd attempted to rape her. In fact that's probably what she's telling the police in St James at this very moment. Where the hell does that leave me, I ask you?'

'Go round to the front. The door's open. We'll talk in the library,' said Lyle. 'Turn left at the end of the hall and it's the first door along. I'll be there myself in a moment.'

He turned and saw Sarah standing in the doorway behind him. After a pause all he said was, 'You shouldn't be standing on those feet.'

Then he walked past her into the bedroom and she thought he was going to leave her there. But he wasn't making for the other door in order to join Terence downstairs. He wanted the dark red silk robe which was hanging from a hook on the back of it.

'Put this on,' he told Sarah, bringing it to her.

It was impossible to tell from his expression whether he believed Terence's story.

'Be quick now.' He turned his back.

She let the towel fall to the floor and hurriedly shrugged

on the robe and wrapped it around her. It was far too big. It engulfed her.

Lyle turned and, as if she were a child, began to roll up the sleeves for her. That done, he picked up the towel and tossed it over his desk chair. Then, putting one arm round her shoulders and the other at the back of her knees, he hoisted her high against his chest.

Dreading the confrontation with the man waiting down in the library, longing to deny his story and yet fearful of the consequences if she did, Sarah lay in Lyle's arms and wondered miserably what Terence would say when he saw her.

CHAPTER NINE

AT first the Irishman looked stupefied. He watched Lyle lower her into a chair, his mouth slack with incredulity. Then relief replaced disbelief.

'Thank God you're all right!' he exclaimed. 'It's a wonder I haven't had a heart attack, the scare you gave me, jumping over the side like that!'

'Why did you jump overboard, Sarah?'

Lyle looked down at her from his position midway between them. His arms were folded across his broad chest. His face was completely impassive.

She swallowed and licked her dry lips. 'It's as he told you . . . I panicked.' She kept her eyes downcast, afraid that if she looked at the other man her scorn and dislike would be visible.

With judicial detachment, Lyle said, 'Not like you to panic without reason, I shouldn't have thought. Are you sure you did no more than kiss her?'—this to Terence.

'I've sworn it once. If you like to hand me a Bible, I'll swear it again on the Good Book. Not one other thing did I do to her.'

'True or false, Sarah?' Lyle asked.

'True,' she replied, in a low tone. 'But it's not true that I led him on. He's nearer my father's age than mine. I only agreed to go sailing because Dudley and Jeff were going as well. Even when they were sidetracked, I expected them to join us for lunch.'

'But in the absence of the young bucks, even an old goat of my age was better than no one to flirt with, eh, my pretty spalpeen?' Terence's tone was quite jovial. 'However, all's well that ends well. I shall be more wary in future, and no doubt you've learnt a lesson.'

'She's not going to be able to walk comfortably for quite some time,' Lyle said sharply. Suddenly he was no longer the aloof arbitrator, but a cold-eyed prosecuting counsel. 'This isn't the first time you've annoyed one of the girls on my staff, Terence. It had better be the last. A man of your age should stick to women in his own league.'

As he spoke, he walked to the glass door giving on to the terrace and, holding it open, said curtly, 'Stay there, Sarah. I shan't be long. Terence!'

With a glowering scowl in her direction, the advertisement manager obeyed the command to withdraw. As the door closed behind him, he began to bluster, his words muted by the glass door and almost immediately quashed by a visibly crushing response from the taller man.

Sarah watched them move across the terrace and disappear down the steps to the cove where Terence must have anchored. She was surprised that he hadn't reached Emerald Hill before her. Presumably he had spent some time cogitating before deciding on a course of action.

His first sheepish admission of being in some part to blame had been a clever and persuasive strategy which might have come off had Lyle been unaware of the pass he had once made at Vashti.

Yet, glad as she was that Lyle had not believed Terence's accusations against her, Sarah could not be happy about the rift which must surely result from an angry dressing down.

Nobody liked to be told off and, in view of the psychotically-strong prejudices seething under the surface of his Irish charm, Terence would resent it more than most. She wondered if Lyle had any suspicion of the other man's secret detestation of the people among whom he worked. No wonder he had not bought her cottage.

Emotionally and physically exhausted, she leaned back in the old high-backed wing chair, one of a pair Lyle had acquired, and looked at the almost empty bookshelves which must once have been crowded with fine leather bindings, and now were waiting to be refilled with his collection of books about the island.

She had heard him mention to Ray that antiquarian booksellers in Europe and in America were keeping him posted about all memoirs, histories and early maps appertaining to Compostela which came into their hands.

It was not more than four or five minutes before he reentered the room, his face less taut with annoyance than it had been when he left it, but still with a hint of displeasure in the set of his mouth.

'I should like your feet to be checked by a doctor before I run you home,' he said. 'We'll wait until Amy comes back. She can lend you some clothes.'

He sat down in the other wing chair and adopted one of his most characteristic 'off duty' positions; his right ankle balanced on his left knee and loosely clasped by his left hand.

'Lyle, I'm sorry I've been instrumental in causing a row between you and Terence,' said Sarah, her tawny eyes troubled.

He didn't reply, but stood up and went to a bookcase which was locked and in which, behind a metal grille, he was keeping a collection of tapes. Having selected one of them, he fitted it on to a tape recorder. The library housed his music centre, and all his recording apparatus.

For a minute or two he played the tape at a speed which made it, to her ears, a meaningless jumble of high-pitched sound. Then he stopped it, and adjusted the speed.

Astonished, she listened to a playback of part of her first conversation with him.

'*I'm afraid I'm not interested, Mr Talbot. I won't waste any more of your time, or my time.*'

'*Stop flapping and sit down, Miss Graham. There would be no extraneous duties of the kind you appear to have in mind. Your*

*condition—which you have confirmed by jumping to the wrong
conclusion, and panicking—is a disadvantage because I need a girl
reporter who won't lose her heart or her head, as virgins are apt to do
until they acquire some wisdom. I shall have more pressing preoccupations than to keep a fatherly eye on you when the local wolves
start to prowl. As inevitably, they will—black and white.'*

Lyle stopped the tape and removed it from the machine.

'I engaged you knowing the hazards. On my own head
be it,' he said dryly.

'I—I thought it was illegal to record people's voices
without their knowledge.'

He shrugged. 'It's a useful technique when interviewing
a large number of candidates. By obviating voluminous
notes, it allows one to concentrate on visual impressions. All
the other recordings were erased as soon as they'd served
their purpose.'

'Why have you kept that one?' she asked.

'Perhaps as a reminder that I had only myself to blame if
this kind of trouble arose.'

Lyle put it away, re-locked the bookcase and, returning
to where he had been sitting, leaned his arms on the back of
the chair.

'Although I'm beginning to wonder if, in calling you an
impressionable virgin, I should have been nearer the mark
had I said a professional virgin.'

Sarah tensed, and lifted her chin. 'What do you mean?'

'There are girls who find it amusing to see how far they
can go without making a man lose control. Teasing is the
polite name for it. It's a dangerous game, and it can be
played once too often—as perhaps it was this afternoon.'

'That's not true. I did nothing—absolutely nothing—to
make Terence behave as he did.'

Slowly his dark eyes appraised her, making her suddenly
conscious of being naked under the silk robe.

'Except that, by looking as you do, you automatically
turn a man's thoughts in that direction. A whole day alone

on a boat with a lovely girl in a bikini is a test of any man's restraint, unless he's happily married, which Terence is not.'

'If I'd realised we would be alone, I shouldn't have gone. I'm beginning to think it was Terence who was playing games when he said the others would be joining us for lunch. If they really were on to something big, how is it they haven't let you in on it?'

'I haven't been near a telephone today. For all I know they may have tried to get in touch with me.'

There was a silence in which he continued to fix her with that curiously unnerving scrutiny. It reminded her of going through Customs on her holidays abroad with her parents, and feeling irrationally guilty although there was nothing in their luggage that they should have declared. Lyle's gaze gave her the same sensation of unjustified uneasiness.

At last, to break the awkward silence, she said, 'If you really think that's what I am—a girl who tries to make fools of men—nothing I can say will convince you otherwise. But I thought you would be more fair-minded than to judge me on circumstantial evidence. What happened today, and the fact that Roddy flew out here, and also your own supposition that Dudley is more than my sailing instructor, don't add up to a watertight case, or not one my father would accept.'

A gleam of mockery lit his eyes. 'You're forgetting something. There have been moments when you and I have been on a closer footing than our professional one. If you weren't leading me on when you were so . . . compliant in my arms, is it fair to conclude you were willing to go a good deal further?'

Her cheeks burned. She lowered her lashes. Here, at last, was the moment of truth when she had to commit herself, one way or the other. Unaware of the movements of her fingers, she toyed with the red silk tassels at the end of the cord of his robe.

'Yes . . . you could conclude that,' she answered, in a low tone. Then, raising her eyes to meet his, 'I've finished redecorating my cottage. Would you like to come to dinner one evening and see the changes I've made?'

'I should be delighted,' said Lyle. 'But perhaps we should postpone it for a few days until your feet are back to normal.' He straightened. 'That sounds like a car coming. I'll go and see who it is.'

On his way to the door, he checked. 'I see no point in publicising what happened this afternoon. It might be advisable to explain the condition of your feet by saying that you trod on some broken glass. The scratches won't be too noticeable when you have clothes on.'

'How shall I account for having to borrow some clothes from Amy?'

Lyle considered. 'Did you see anyone you knew today?' She shook her head.

'Then we can give the impression that you were with me. In our haste to get your feet dressed, we left your clothes at the beach. I shall pick them up later—as indeed I shall, but from Terence's boat.'

'Won't that give rise to some gossip?—Our spending a beach day together.'

'Perhaps—but it's inevitable anyway. You don't imagine that a close relationship between us will pass unnoticed, do you?'

'I suppose not.'

'Impossible, Sarah,' he said dryly. 'Such things, if not common knowledge, are always known to one's intimates, which, in our case, means all our colleagues. Does that make you change your mind? Shall you dislike being linked with me?'

Again she shook her head. Lyle's mouth curved slightly, then he left the room.

Shortly afterwards Amy appeared, carrying some clothes over her arm.

'I'm sorry to hear about your accident, Sarah,' she said. 'Are your feet very painful?'

'No, not very. Lyle has bandaged them up to look a lot worse than they are. Thanks, Amy. I hope you don't mind my borrowing your clothes for a short time?'

'Don't be silly! Of course not. I've brought down a skirt and top, and a pair of briefs. My bras would be too big for you, but the top isn't tight, so you won't need one.'

She helped Sarah put on her things. 'Ted and Lyle are making tea and sandwiches. Tea's a great reviver after something nasty has happened. Doesn't it infuriate you?— People being so lazy and careless that they can't be bothered to take their litter home with them. Paper and plastic are bad enough, but glass is downright dangerous. Which beach were you at when it happened?'

'I don't know the name of it.' Sarah was a bad liar. Even white lies—other than those to spare people's feelings— made her feel uncomfortable.

Fortunately Amy didn't ask any more questions, but went on to describe her day out with Ted. Presently the two men joined them, and about half an hour later Lyle carried Sarah back to the car.

The visit to the doctor, whom Lyle had rung up in advance to make sure he was at home, did not take long. The doctor complimented him on his efficient first aid, and told him to bring her back if there was any sign of inflammation.

'But you look very healthy, young lady. I should say you'll be back in high heels by this time next week,' he told Sarah.

By this time she was growing accustomed to being swung up in Lyle's strong arms.

'Your feet will heal a lot faster if you don't come to work tomorrow, and keep them off the ground as much as possible,' he said, as he carried her from the surgery to where he had left the car. 'I'll bring you a take-away lunch, and take you out to dinner, so you won't need to bother with cooking. Are you up to eating out tonight? Or are you exhausted?'

'Exhausted? No! Do I seem such a frail creature to you?'

He lowered her carefully into the passenger seat.

'No, quite the reverse. Most girls would have been in tears, if not hysterics, after what you went through this afternoon.'

When he took his place behind the wheel and pulled his seat belt from the reel, she said, 'I nearly did cry just after you gave me a lift. If you'd badgered me then, I should have dissolved.'

It was dark when he carried her to the cottage, but a lot of the residents of the street were still sitting out on their porches, including both sets of neighbours.

By the time she had answered their sympathetic enquiries, and introduced them to Lyle, she was beginning to feel very weary.

When the joiner's wife told her she ought to go to bed, and offered to bring round some supper, Sarah would have refused. But Lyle said, 'That's a good idea, Mrs Rogers. I was going to take her out to eat, but a light meal at home and an early night will do her more good. I'll see you at lunch-time tomorrow, Sarah.'

About two hours later, when her kindly neighbours had stopped fussing over her, she locked her front door and climbed into bed. How many more nights would she spend on her own before the night came when she had to prove that her eager response to Lyle's kisses had not been an act of false promise?

The next day he brought back her beach bag, and the clothes she had worn to go sailing.

The lunch he provided was delicious, and accompanied by a bottle of wine. They ate it on her pint-sized porch which was just large enough for a table for two, and two chairs.

'By the way, Dudley and Jeff spent the whole of yesterday snorkelling,' he told her, while they ate. 'They had two girls with them; Dudley's sister, and a friend of hers in whom, I gather, he has a more than friendly interest. It seems I was wrong in thinking he had his eye on you. Regrettably, it also suggests that Terence's behaviour was not unpremeditated. He must have had it in mind from the outset.'

'Perhaps he thought I wouldn't rebuff him . . . that it wouldn't be necessary to . . . be so unpleasant. I think he may be a vain man who imagines he's irresistible. He must, to have made a pass at Vashti.'

'You knew about that?'

'I was near his office one day when I heard a slap and then she stalked out in high dudgeon. But it was a long time ago. I'd more or less forgotten it.'

'He'll have to be replaced,' said Lyle.

'Isn't that rather drastic? After what you said to him yesterday, he's hardly likely to start pestering Gloria.'

'Supposing you hadn't been able to jump into the sea and swim for it yesterday? What then?'

'I—I don't know what would have happened. But I'm prepared to give him the benefit of the doubt.'

'I'm not,' said Lyle, in a cold tone. 'On a personal level I have difficulty in keeping my hands off him. Professionally, I have other reasons for thinking him better replaced. Although he's been careful to hide it, I suspect that Terence has ideas which have no place in any civilised society, and particularly not in a predominantly black milieu. A few days ago I heard him speaking to Gary in a way I didn't like. If Gary's colour had nothing to do with it, it was still not the way I expect to hear any of my staff addressing someone in a junior position.'

'Can you replace him?' she asked.

'No one is indispensable—not even my girl reporter,' he added, his expression losing its severity and becoming warmer, and faintly teasing as he said, 'We'll go inside now, shall we? I sense that a Peeping Thomasina is keeping watch on us from the house opposite and, although I daresay she'd enjoy it, I think we'll deny her the interest of looking on while I——'

He paused, his eyes on her mouth, and Sarah felt her heart jerk with excitement.

'—check your feet,' he finished prosaically.

'Oh . . .' A gurgle of laughter broke from her. 'How unromantic! I thought——' She stopped, suddenly shy.

'That, too. But duty before pleasure. I'll clear the table. You hobble inside to the sofa.'

She did as he bade her. But when the table was cleared, he did not close the front door as she expected. Nobody passing could see them, but anyone coming to the door would.

To examine her feet, he sat on the studio couch with his back to her, like a farrier inspecting a horse's hooves, she thought with a touch of vexation that the consummation of their relationship had to be deferred until her feet had healed. Why must they wait? Waiting made her nervous . . . uncertain of doing the right thing. Was she letting her body make a fool of her?

Yet just the sight of his black head bent over her feet, the width of his shoulders stretching the fabric of his shirt, made her weak with longing to feel that powerful back bow to the pressure of her outspread hands.

'They're coming along well. As the doctor said, you're young and healthy.' Lyle finished replacing the dressings and turned to face her. 'And very beautiful.'

She was leaning against the mass of cushions which, by day, made the studio couch look less bed-like.

He drew her to him and kissed her. After a moment she ceased to be passive in his arms, and slid her own round his neck, pressing her softness against him, hoping the warmth of her response would excite him beyond his power to restrain himself, and put an end to her suspense.

But Lyle, although he kissed her long and fiercely, had a greater control over himself than Terence or Roddy.

Eventually he put her away from him and, breathing hard, his eyes alight with desire, said huskily, 'Are you so impatient to fathom the mystery?'

'Yes . . . yes,' she whispered. 'Oh, Lyle . . .'—attempting to draw him back to her.

He held her off, and shook his head. 'This is not the time—or the place.'

Too swept by emotion to dissemble, she blurted, 'But that's why I wanted the cottage. Somewhere small . . . the wrong side of the tracks . . . where no one would take any notice of your visits to me.'

'A love-nest, eh? The Compostelan equivalent of one of those little houses in St John's Wood where Edwardian rakes kept their mistresses about the turn of the century?'

'Don't tease me! It isn't so foolish. You have your position to think of. Here, we shan't be noticed by anyone who matters.'

'But we shall be noticed. And people who matter, as you put it, have people who don't working for them. Gossip spreads as fast as a scrub fire. Already that old girl in the house opposite has probably timed our disappearance, and is now surmising—quite correctly—that we're up to something improper.'

'What's improper about a little kissing?' She indulged a long-suppressed wish to smooth the tip of her forefinger along his mouth. 'And the front door is open. It couldn't be more respectable.'

He captured her hand and pressed his mouth into the palm.

'But what you are doing to me, and what I should like to do to you, is not respectable, my little siren. If you're determined to toss your bonnet over the windmill, it has to be somewhere else, not here.'

Her face fell. 'But where can we go?'

'I'll think about it. Perhaps, by the time I come for you this evening, I'll have worked out a plan for a few days' seclusion together. I'll be back at seven. We'll have dinner at the Green Parrot.'

Sarah spent the afternoon in a ferment of uncertainty. The idea of a relationship which could only be carried on at irregular intervals was much less acceptable to her than the way she had visualised their affair.

A love-nest was somehow cosier and less cheapening than snatched weekends in hotels or holiday apartments where always there would be a risk of meeting people they knew.

She would have liked to slip into town and buy herself a new dress. She didn't want Lyle to be reminded of the previous occasion when she had worn the leaf-scattered honey voile.

Then she remembered Raine's churidars, and shocking pink shirt, brought from London, which would go with them.

'You don't need to carry me tonight. It doesn't hurt me to walk slowly,' she said, when he came to collect her.

'As you wish.' He offered her his arm. 'It's all arranged. We're both having the whole of next week off.'

'The whole week? But what will the others think?'

'They'll think you're staying with your parents on their visit to Antigua, and that I'm seeing my sister and brother-in-law. Ray can write the first and second leaders, and edit the paper in my absence, and you can write the women's page in advance.'

'And where shall we really be going?'

'To Antigua. I've booked a secluded house which is generally rented to honeymooners—which is what we shall be . . . in effect.'

In effect. But not in reality.

'It sounds lovely. What fun,' she said brightly.

But there was an ache in her throat for the infinitely lovelier might-have-been; the happy beginning of a future inseparably linked; the total, unqualified commitment to love forever and a day.

The Green Parrot was a restaurant in one of St James's old, balconied, weatherboard houses. Their table was near a slow-whirling three-bladed ceiling fan from which pleasant eddies of cool air came their way without disturbing the flame of the glass-shaded candle between them.

They were the first people there, and the proprietor came to chat to them about his menu, which included specialities from all the islands. They chose rabbit with prunes, a Martinique dish, with the rabbit marinated in red wine and thyme for a day and a night before being cooked with onions and bacon, celery, rum and the wine-swollen prunes.

'My great-grandmother came from Martinique.'

Sarah told Lyle the story of Marie-Martine, disowned by her rich Creole parents for allying herself with a young man they could never accept.

'I'm supposed to inherit my eyes from her,' she added.

'And your reckless, romantic nature, I shouldn't wonder. Fortunately, nowadays, parents rarely if ever disown their daughters.'

'No, but they can still be hurt by their children's actions. I—I shan't tell mine about us. They liked you, but they wouldn't like knowing that we . . . that we were lovers.'

'And it goes against the grain with you, I fancy. Yet you're still determined to go through with it. Why?'

As he spoke, he reached for her hand, which was resting on the edge of the table, and took it gently in his, stroking her palm with his thumb.

Because I love you. Because the summit of my existence will be the nights I spend in your arms.

Aloud, she said lightly, 'No one can stay "an impression-able virgin" for ever. Why was it that you didn't invite me to become one of your sub-tenants at Emerald Hill? Because you foresaw that we might become . . . closer than colleagues?'

'Yes.'

'So much for your assurance that there would be "no extraneous duties of the kind you appear to have in mind",' she said, quoting the tape-recording.

'I was referring to the sort of situation where a man in a higher position puts pressure on a girl to be nice to him—or else. As far as our relationship is concerned, we shall have to try and separate our working lives from our private life, the way people do who are married and work together.'

Not a very diplomatic comparison, she thought, with a pang. Surely he must guess that what she longed for was marriage?

'I—I thought you were going to make love to me the day you insisted on coming to look at the cottage, and then your sister arrived unexpectedly, and we didn't go to the beach after all.'

Lyle lifted an eyebrow. 'You seriously thought I would make love to you on a public beach? You don't give me credit for much finesse. Or does love al fresco appeal to your romanticism more than anything as conventional as a double bed?'

'Hush . . . someone might hear,' she murmured, with a nervous glance at the people at nearby tables.

'In that case I'll take you for a drive, and find somewhere where we can discuss these interesting topics more freely,' he said, with a teasing gleam.

The hood of his car, which he kept up during the day to shade the interior, tonight was in its folded position. Although she had often envied Vashti her long, straight hair, one advantage of Sarah's little-boy short crop was that nothing disarranged it. She could enjoy the night breeze blowing back from the windscreen without being concerned that, by the end of the drive, she would be unflatteringly dishevelled.

Lyle took her to Indian Point, a publicly owned headland where there was little vegetation other than goat-cropped turf. The beauty of the place lay in the pounding of the surf against the rocks, each wave tossing up veils of spray.

'Good. We have it to ourselves,' said Lyle, as he switched off the engine and the lights. 'Have you been here before?'

'Only once—in the daytime, by myself,' she added, in case he should think she had been to the Point with Jeff or Dudley. 'Before I had the cottage to occupy me, I was working my way round the coast, trying to see all the places of interest. This was the site of a Carib settlement, I believe.'

'Yes, but I didn't bring you here to discuss the archaeological finds.'

He moved along the bench seat to draw her close, and say quietly, 'You haven't answered my question.'

'W-what question?'

The tone of his voice, the easy assurance with which he took her in his arms, the sense of a potent force held in check, but perhaps not for long, all conspired to make her own voice unsteady.

His lips brushed her temple and cheek, stopping short of her mouth.

'Do you want to see the sky when you open your eyes—after I make a woman of you?'

Without waiting for her answer, he began to kiss her.

His kisses were like the powerful surge of the waves. She wasn't a strong enough swimmer to survive those turbulent breakers, nor had she the power to resist the surging emotions he aroused in her.

'No, no . . . oh, Lyle, *please* . . . not here. Someone might come,' she gasped, when at last he allowed her to speak.

'No, not here,' he agreed, with a soft laugh. 'But it could be arranged, if there's a streak of the gypsy in you.'

'You . . . you make me feel like a . . . a pagan. I—I don't know myself,' she whispered, her traitorous hands sliding over his shoulders, while the faint voice of common sense told her that it was madness to beg him to stop and then to caress his strong neck with the tips of her fingers.

'Your skin tastes like honey,' he murmured, his lips to her throat. 'This time next week we shall be in bed together. Are you as impatient as I am? You are, aren't you, Sarah?'

'*Yes . . . yes!*' she breathed, arching her neck.

What was she saying? How could she freely admit it?—to a man who had never said he loved her.

But nor had she said she loved him, and she did—oh, God, how she did!

He unbuttoned the shocking pink shirt and drew aside the soft silk to expose her small, dark-tipped breasts. The breeze felt cool on her flesh, but his hands and his lips were warm, and almost unbearably exciting. Sarah drew in deep shuddering breaths and expelled them in rapturous sighs, aware of a sharp ache of longing deep down in her body.

When his lips returned to her mouth, there was no resistance left in her. Even the passionate kisses which had made her recoil from Roddy were different when she was in Lyle's arms. With him, nothing could offend her.

It was he who brought to an end those moments of shattering abandonment.

'Time I took you home.' His voice was thick with desire.

All the way back to St James, and while he carried her from the car to the gate of her cottage, she felt sure he had changed his mind and meant to stay the night with her. But instead he set her on her feet, kissing the tip of her nose, and strode rather briskly away. She watched him depart with mixed feelings.

She hoped it wasn't only his wish to avoid causing gossip which was making him leave her. He must have tremendous self-control. She felt certain that his urge to take her had been every whit as strong as the lust which had driven Terence to behave like a brute on his boat.

So why had Lyle held in check the impelling force she had sensed in him? Only for her sake, not his. Only, perhaps, because he wanted to make the first time as perfect as possible for her—short of making her his wife.

Or was she deluding herself?

The days remaining before their departure gave her many uncomfortable moments. She felt sure the others must think it a curious coincidence that she and Lyle should be taking leave at the same time.

'How long are your parents staying?' Vashti asked her.

'I'm not sure,' was Sarah's embarrassed answer.

Why should a man with boyhood associations with Compostela, and a daughter working there, choose to spend a holiday in Antigua? She felt sure that question must have occurred to Vashti, and to the other members of the editorial staff.

Lyle's cover-story was more plausible. She had heard him telling his chief reporter that in a recent letter from Paul, his brother-in-law had sounded increasingly dissatisfied with life in the American capital, and envious of the more leisurely pace in St James.

'The time may be ripe to suggest a change to him,' Lyle had said to Ray.

But it was, Sarah guessed, a suggestion which would be made by letter, not in person.

When the day came for them to leave, she was thankful to get away. Half-truths and evasive answers were as little to her liking as black lies.

After landing on the larger island, they took a taxi

from the airport to the house Lyle was renting. As it was some way from the shops, he had arranged for a hired car to be delivered to them the following morning.

The cab-driver was a middle-aged man who still used the old form of address to his women passengers.

'Mind your head, mistress,' he said to Sarah, as he opened the rear door for her.

In other circumstances the old-fashioned courtesy would have charmed her. Today, it touched a raw nerve. As the taxi moved forward she turned her face to the window, blinking back sudden tears.

Mistress. Girl-friend. Whatever one called what she was about to become, it didn't sound at all permanent.

The house was much larger than she had expected it to be. It was built on a knoll to catch every whisper of breeze, overlooking a creek where a few boats were moored. The nearest beach, so Lyle had been told, was a five-minute dawdle from the garden.

The house had verandahs on all sides, a huge, airy living-room, three spacious double bedrooms and two single rooms used by the owners' teenage children.

'Which of the bedrooms do you prefer?' Lyle asked, having looked at them all.

The visitors' bedrooms were no less luxurious than the master bedroom. All three had adjoining bathrooms, king-size beds, and the kind of décor achieved only by a professional designer, or a woman with exceptionally stylish taste.

'I think the green and white room,' said Sarah, opting for the one in which walls, curtains, bedhead and bedcover were all white glazed chintz latticed with fresh apple green. 'But I don't really mind. Which do you like?'

'Any bedroom with you in it would please me.'

He put his arm round her and, for the first time that day, his mouth came down warmly on hers.

At first the intensity of her shyness made her stiffen instead of yielding. But, with his usual assurance, Lyle knew how to deal with that. Using his height to sway her backwards, he caused her instinctively to cling to him. At once the close contact of their bodies melted her resistance.

It would not have surprised her to be made love to before they had even unpacked. But after a while, with obvious reluctance, he let her go; and because she wanted to be perfect for him—cool from the shower, her skin silky and scented with the delicate fragrance of a very expensive French body lotion—she did not make any gesture which might have altered his decision.

'As there's an abundance of bathrooms, we may as well have one apiece. You have the one off the bedroom, and I'll use the one which is shared by the two single rooms. I'll just unpack my shaving and washing gear, and then we'll look at the beach,' he said, as he picked up her suitcase and carried it to the bedroom she had chosen.

It did not take Sarah long to unpack her small case. She had brought a minimal wardrobe of mix-match beachwear, two after-dark dresses, and the apricot night-gown. She shook it out and laid it across the bed.

She had changed into one of her bikinis and was putting the case away in a cupboard when Lyle reappeared in his bathing briefs.

'I'll unpack my other stuff later. Let's go.'

There were not more than half a dozen people on the half-mile-long stretch of pink sand which they reached a few minutes later. By the time they emerged from the water, everyone else had disappeared. As it was by now two o'clock, presumably they had all gone back to their houses for lunch.

'Hungry?' asked Lyle, as they walked to where their beach towels were spread in the shade of a sea-grape.

'Not very. Are you?'

'No, but I checked the refrigerator. It's stocked with everything I ordered so that we don't have to eat out tonight.'

Sarah lay down to dry off. Even in the shade, the drops of water on her skin would soon evaporate. The winter climate of the Leeward Islands was not humid and sticky and enervating. The sun could be dangerously hot, especially at this hour of day, but always the horizon was clear and the trade wind rustled the palm fronds.

Their towels were placed close together, and Lyle lay down on his stomach and propped himself on his elbows to look at her upturned face.

'Are you happy, Sarah? No last-minute doubts?'

'Only that, being "an impressionable virgin", I may disappoint you. Otherwise I'm *very* happy.'

He rolled on his side, leaving one hand free to touch the outlines of her face.

'Aren't you worried that, after waiting so long for the experience, it may be you who is disappointed?'

'No. I'm sure you're a wonderful lover.' She captured his hand and cradled it against her cheek, letting love shine in her eyes, even if it could never be uttered.

'When you look at me so trustingly, I begin to lose my nerve,' he said, his smile tinged with wryness. 'What are you expecting, I wonder?'

She touched his strong, forceful chin, her fingernails pale against the darkness of his skin.

She said, for once teasing him, 'Ecstasy! What else?'

'As long as you don't expect the earth to move.'

'What do you mean?'

'You haven't read Hemingway's book *For Whom The Bell Tolls*?'

'No.'

'Good. I once knew a woman correspondent who told me that her generation—by which she meant bookish girls who grew up in the forties—had all been badly disappointed after reading that novel.'

'Why was that?'

'It was about a group of guerilla fighters during the Spanish Civil War. They included an American and a Spanish girl. When he took her into his sleeping-bag and made love to her, she felt the earth move, as she'd been told that it would if he was the right man for her.'

'But it doesn't really?'

'I understand not. There are other manifestations which are less cataclysmic but equally satisfactory, so I'm told.'

He leaned close and began to kiss her. Sarah's eyelids fluttered and closed. His lips tasted salty, as hers must. She felt his hand slip down her throat and along the string of her halter to cover the wisp of damp cotton and the warm skin above her heart.

Some time later the voices of children, still distant but coming their way, made Lyle draw away and sit up. Dazedly, Sarah opened her eyes, seeing the crimson-veined leaves of the sea-grape, and the blue sky, and white clouds scudding, and feeling her body pulsating with delicious sensations which slowly, slowly subsided.

After a while Lyle stood up, and put on his short khaki sarong. 'There's a bottle of champagne waiting for us in the refrigerator.'

They walked back to the house, their hands linked, not speaking, looking at each other. His eyes which, seen very close, were actually the colour of the darkest blackstrap rum and only black at the outer edge of the iris, moved like a possessive caress over her near-naked curves; and she, in turn, gazed at him, delighting in the panther-like symmetry of his tall, supple, muscular frame.

At the house, he unlocked the door and stood aside for her to go in.

'Do you want a quick shower before . . . lunch?'

But it wasn't lunch he had in mind, judging by the gleam in his eyes.

'Yes. I—I shan't be long.' She turned away, inwardly trembling.

At that time of day even turning on the cold tap resulted in a spray of warm water. Gradually it cooled. Sarah was vigorously towelling her hair when a sound from outside made her pause, thinking she had heard a car draw up.

Surely she must have imagined it? If this house was frequently occupied by newlyweds, whoever took care of the property for the owners would scarcely be so inept as to come and enquire after their well-being during the siesta hours.

But it *was* a car, and bringing more than one person. There was no mistaking the sound of at least two voices.

Could it be that, by a careless mistake, the house had been double-booked, and the people arriving were a pair of bona fide honeymooners?

Torn between exasperation and amusement at such a bizarre situation, Sarah wrapped herself in a bath sheet and padded across the green-carpeted bedroom to listen at the door.

CHAPTER TEN

LYLE must have left the door unlocked. She didn't hear the newcomers putting a key in the lock. The first sound she could make out was a West Indian voice saying, 'Thank you very much, sir. Goodbye, mistress. Enjoy your holiday.'

Obviously a taxi-driver, perhaps the same man who had brought them to the house a while ago.

Then, to her stupefaction, she heard a familiar voice say, 'There doesn't seem to be anyone here. Perhaps they weren't expecting us yet, and they're at the beach.'

Sarah gasped and wrenched open the door.

'*Dad!—Mother!* Oh . . . how *wonderful* to see you!'

As her mother held out her arms, she flung herself into them, momentarily forgetting everything but her joy at being reunited with them.

It was a few minutes before the two women were capable of coherent speech; and her father, although he kept his feelings under stricter control, was clearly much moved by the sight of his daughter.

By the time they had begun to recover themselves, Lyle had appeared, clad in a pair of white shorts.

'Your flight must have been dead on time. I'm delighted to see you. How are you, sir?'—shaking hands with her father before turning to her mother, and saying, 'Welcome to the Caribbean, Mrs Graham. I hope this is going to be the first of very many visits.'

'I hope so, too, but none as exciting as this one. I've hardly slept a wink since your call. You've fixed the wedding by now, I expect? When is it to be?' she asked eagerly.

'The day after tomorrow. My sister and her husband

can't get here until tomorrow and, as they're my only close relations, naturally I'd like them to be present.' He turned to Sarah, gave her an impudent wink which they could not see, and put his arm round her shoulders. 'How do you think the bride is looking?'

'Like most brides forty-eight hours before the great day—as if she doesn't know whether she's on her head or her heels,' was her father's smiling comment.

'But still our sweet, pretty Sarah,' said her mother fondly. 'Not a bit changed, I'm glad to see.'

'No, not until Monday,' said Lyle. 'When she stops being Miss Graham and becomes Mrs Talbot.'

His quizzical smile defied her to announce that this was the first she had heard of it.

'I'm sure you're as hot as we were when we first arrived here,' he went on, speaking to her parents. 'Why not unpack your bathing kit and go straight to the beach while Sarah and I fix a snack for ourselves. We haven't had lunch yet. We'll bring it down to the beach in a cool bag, with a bottle appropriate to the occasion.'

'A very sound plan of action, Lyle,' said her father. 'Come along, Mary.'

While Lyle picked up their cases and led the way to the master bedroom, her mother gave Sarah another affectionate hug.

'I can't believe we're here, dear. I'm longing to hear all the details, and to see your wedding dress. When we talked on the telephone, I asked Lyle if we should bring one with us, but he said no, you had it organised.'

A few minutes later, leaving the Grahams to change out of their travelling clothes, Lyle and Sarah went to the large and well-equipped kitchen.

'My mother's impatience to see my wedding dress is nothing to mine,' she said with deceptive mildness, as soon as they were safely out of earshot.

'Raine is bringing it with her tomorrow. You seemed so

much on a wavelength that I felt it was safe to ask her to choose something suitable for a small and very private wedding. The shops in Washington are much better than here, or in St James. Are you angry with me?'

'Angry—no. Merely baffled. What made you suddenly decide to make an honest woman of me?'

'It wasn't a sudden decision. It's been in my mind since I met you. Even before I met you, Bob's wife Maggie told me you were the girl for me. I dismissed it as matchmaking nonsense and dodged her attempts to bring us together. Then you applied for the job I'd advertised, and by the end of the interview I'd a feeling Maggie was right.'

They were standing several yards apart, and he made no attempt to come near her.

'When a man falls in love at first sight, if he has a vestige of sense left he puts off committing himself until he's had time to discover if the girl is as perfect as she seems.'

Her father put his head round the door. 'Ah, here you are. Could I have a word with you in private, Lyle?'

Lyle seemed to hesitate. 'I shan't be long, Sarah.'

'Go ahead.' She bit back the quip about secrets which sprang to her lips.

How could she be annoyed with him for making her believe they were here illicitly, when in fact he had long intended to realise her dearest wish?

He was back within a few minutes, one hand in the pocket of his shorts.

'You once made a remark which gave me a clue to the stone you might choose for your engagement ring. I commissioned your father to bring one over from London for me. If you don't like it, you have only to say so, and it can be changed for something else.'

He took from his pocket a small case, which he opened, showing her what it contained.

'It's gorgeous!' she breathed, her eyes wide with surprise and delight.

He slid the ring over her knuckle, alongside the silver Greek ring on her little finger.

'What did I say to make you guess that I've always longed for an aquamarine?'

'You were talking about colour to Raine, and you said it was one of your favourites—the colour of the shallow water round the islands. I know you like pink and red, and I could have chosen a ruby or a pink diamond. But I like aquamarines myself.'

She turned the stone this way and that. It was a beautiful colour, neither blue nor green but something of each, like the sea.

'You were very sure I loved you, Lyle.'

'Latterly, yes. As sure as of my love for you. It's not only for love that women give themselves to men, but with you there could be no other reason.'

He raised her hand to his lips and kissed her fingers before he said, 'Perhaps it was a little unfair of me to mislead you about the nature of our stay here. But you're very engaging when you're trying to play the sophisticate, and proving enchantingly miscast.'

'I think it was monstrous of you,' she told him, without much conviction. 'It would have served you right if I'd chickened out at the last moment. My parents would revise their good opinion of you if they knew the ostensible reason for our trip here. I'm sure my father would regard seducing a female employee as every bit as bad as embezzlement.'

'But I haven't seduced you, my sweet girl,' said Lyle, as he put his arms round her. 'You're still as innocent as most parents hope their daughters will be on their wedding day, but as they very rarely are. But not for much longer . . .' he murmured, crushing her to him, his mouth demanding a foretaste of total surrender.

'What an idyllic spot!' exclaimed Mrs Graham, when they joined her parents on the beach. 'Sarah dear, I forgot to ask about your feet. Lyle explained that you'd had an accident which prevented you coming to the phone when he rang up to tell us your news. He said it was nothing serious. But what happened exactly?'

'I—I trod on some glass at the beach. They're better now.' Sarah showed the soles of her feet, still marked but otherwise healed.

While they shared a bottle of champagne, her father said, 'What would you like for a wedding present? As you aren't having the kind of wedding that gives the father of the bride nightmares, we'd like to give you something substantial.'

'Can we think about it?' asked Sarah.

It crossed her mind that a present which would give them both pleasure would be a sailing dinghy. Her father was not so wealthy that he could afford to give them a boat of the kind that Lyle had sacrificed for the newspaper, but she felt sure her husband-to-be would not despise a more modest vessel in which he could impart some of his superior skills to her.

'Where are you going for your honeymoon?' her mother asked.

'I don't know. Lyle is keeping it a secret. He's a very secretive man,' she replied, with an impish grin at him.

'I've only just finalised the details. As Sarah has been learning to sail, and as many of the finest beaches are only accessible by sea, I've chartered a bareboat. That's a boat without a crew,' he explained. 'We'll be away for a week, and then we'll come back and collect you'—speaking to her parents—'and take you across to Compostela to spend the remainder of your holiday at Emerald Hill.'

That evening, while all four of them were in the kitchen, drinking some more champagne and preparing a meal, the telephone rang. It was Lyle's sister, calling from Washington. He had a chat with her first, then handed the receiver to Sarah.

'Darling Sarah, I couldn't be more pleased,' Raine's voice said warmly, from America. 'But I do think it's too bad of Lyle not to give you the time to fly up here and choose your trousseau. However, I've found you a wedding dress in which you'll look quite irresistible. It's white chiffon, hemmed with white silk, and I'm bringing organdie daisies for you to wear in your hair, and praying that you take a size five because I've bought you some sandals. They're the "something blue"—pale blue kid.'

She would have chattered on indefinitely, but eventually a pleasant male voice intervened.

'Sarah? Hello. This is Paul—soon to be your brother-in-law. If I don't stop my garrulous wife, she'll be on the line half the night! You can talk your heads off tomorrow. We'll see you around noon. Goodbye now.'

The call reminded Lyle that he had some prints of the photographs taken during Raine's previous visit. He fetched them to show to the Grahams. Sarah had forgotten about them—the snap she had taken of brother and sister, the snaps he had taken of her with Raine, and the one snapped by Raine of herself perched on his long strong thigh.

'That's a portent, if ever I saw one. Don't you think so, John?' asked Mrs Graham as she handed this last to her husband.

'I think you're right,' he said, smiling.

'May I see?' Sarah held out her hand.

Remembering how Raine had instructed her to put her arm on Lyle's shoulders, she thought it must be her expression which had given the game away. But in fact she was staring into space, her face misleadingly aloof. It was Lyle whom the camera had caught with his innermost feelings exposed.

He was looking at her with a mixture of tenderness and desire. If only she had known how he felt then, how much heartache it would have saved her!

Predictably, soon after supper her parents retired to their room, overcome by the uncontrollable yawns of travellers through several time zones.

'Shall we go for a stroll?' Lyle suggested.

It was full moon. A perfect night. They took off their sandals and splashed, hand in hand, through the shallows, sometimes over smooth sea-washed sand as a wave receded, sometimes instep-deep in silver foam.

No one else was there at that hour. They had the beach to themselves, as if they were two happy castaways on an island as remote as Robinson Crusoe's.

Presently, a little uncertainly, Sarah said,

'I know there must have been many other women in your life, but that's all in the past and doesn't concern me. But I should like to know your side of the story about you and Rosemary.'

'Rosemary?' he said blankly.

'Jack's wife. She was my predecessor at the time when you worked on the *News*.'

'Oh, yes, Rosemary. Who regaled you with that ancient history?'

'She did—Rosemary herself. I was at her house one evening, and you came on the box, and she switched off. Then it all came out . . . your love affair with her, and how you had ditched her—or so she said.'

'And you believed her?'

'At the time, yes. Not any more. Knowing you, I can't believe you would ever walk out of anyone's life without saying goodbye or explaining why you were leaving.'

'No, I didn't do that, but I can't exculpate myself of all responsibility for that débâcle. I hope Rosemary is never so foolish as to confide our connection to her husband. He probably knows she had several lovers before he married her, but he might not take kindly to my being among them,' Lyle said sardonically.

He stopped, turning Sarah to face him, and tilting her face up to the moonlight.

'It was a long time ago, ten years ago, and it wasn't a love affair. There was precious little tenderness between us. Maybe she's calmed down now, after eight or nine years of marriage and a couple of kids, but in those days Rosemary was riding the Women's Lib band-wagon. If she fancied a man, she told him so and invited him back to her bed-sitter. I don't mean to imply she was an unduly promiscuous girl. She wasn't. She was merely behaving in the way the male sex have always behaved at that age.'

He stopped looking down into her eyes, and began to walk on.

'I don't think Rosemary was attracted to me in the usual sense. It was partly an extension of her desire to flout all the conventions of her parents' generation. They were a very narrow-minded, bigoted couple who had had trouble with all their children. I hope, when you and I have children, we'll have the sense to strike the happy medium between no discipline and too much.'

'Do you want to emulate your sister, and have a large family?'

'That's something we'll have to work out between us. For the next few years I should prefer to have you to myself. Just the two of us, until you're in your mid-twenties. But there again it depends on what you want.'

'I should like the same thing as you—to be your wife for a few years before becoming a mother.'

Sarah would have been content to drop the subject of the other woman. Suddenly she wasn't curious any more.

But after a pause, Lyle went on, 'I believe it gave Rosemary some kind of kick to feel that certain people were looking disapprovingly at us when we went about in public together. Eventually she carried sex equality to its logical conclusion and asked me to marry her. I imagine it's that, more than anything else, which she finds it galling to remember.'

'It must always be terribly wounding to have a proposal turned down, the more so when a girl has reversed the traditional roles. I feel embarrassed about admitting to you the reason why I bought Cordia Cottage. But at least you had already made it clear that you wanted to make love to me,' said Sarah. 'She must have loved you, Lyle, even if you didn't feel the same way.'

'It could never have worked. I'm not opposed to mixed marriages. One has only to look at Vashti, who has African, European, Indian and Chinese blood in her, to see what superb human beings can result from a blending of races. But, in an imperfect world, a marriage between people of different colours does call for exceptional strength of character,' he said gravely. 'Or the kind of total rapport which Rosemary and I never had, but which I think you and I do.'

Again he stopped, and turned her to him.

'Had we been of different races, I couldn't have held out against you. It isn't only your lovely face which delights me. It's your smile—and the things which make you smile. It's even your attitude to your job, and the way you fit in with your colleagues. You're a sweet person, Sarah. A darling. You could make a lot of men happy.'

His praise made her feel like purring. After the weeks of uncertainty, of feeling he would never truly care for her, it would be a long time—if ever—before she could take his love for granted.

Lyle folded her close in his arms and, with her cheek against his chest, and his tall head bent over hers, he said softly, 'Beauty is a variable concept, and I happen to find everything about you beautiful. But all the other, more important things which a man looks for in a woman—gentleness, loyalty, encouragement—they're universal. I should have had to love you, no matter what you looked like.'

'*When you were a king in Babylon, and I was a Christian slave* . . .' Sarah murmured dreamily.

A ripple washed over their feet as they stood, embraced, in the moonlight. The sea was as warm as by day, but at night it had the colourless clarity of crystal instead of being aquamarine as it was in the daytime.

She thought of her French great-grandmother who, on an island to the south, perhaps had slipped out at night to meet her stalwart young lover on a beach as lovely as this one.

They had had everything against them—her whiteness, his blackness, the rigid social barriers of their lifetime.

But love knew no boundaries, no rules. For centuries, people had been falling in love in defiance of all prohibitions. Some, like Francesca and Paolo, had brought tragedy upon themselves. Others, such as her great-grandparents, had lived out their lives in unrecorded happiness.

Perhaps he had looked something like Lyle. Tall and powerful, with amused dark eyes which had made Marie-Martine quiver inside when he looked at her.

Like Lyle, he must have had a good brain as well as a strong body. For although he had been descended from generations of slaves, and had had little opportunity to improve his own lot, his son had been an educated man, his grandson had become a lawyer, and his great-granddaughter was a journalist of, she hoped, the more responsible kind.

'How lucky we are. We have nothing against us, and everything going for us,' she said contentedly. 'A lovely house to live in, a shared interest in the paper, swimming . . . sailing . . .'

Lyle felt for her chin and turned her face up to his. 'This . . .' he said, his voice suddenly husky.

As his mouth took possession of hers, igniting the instant response he could always arouse in her, she had one swift glimpse of the stars before her eyes closed in ecstasy.

How to join in a whole new world of romance

It's very easy to subscribe to the Mills & Boon Reader Service. As a regular reader, you can enjoy a whole range of special benefits. Bargain offers. Big cash savings. Your own free Reader Service newsletter, packed with knitting patterns, recipes, competitions, and exclusive book offers.

We send you the very latest titles each month, postage and packing free – no hidden extra charges. There's absolutely no commitment – you receive books for only as long as you want.

We'll send you details. Simply send the coupon – or drop us a line for details about the Mills & Boon Reader Service Subscription Scheme. Post to: Mills & Boon Reader Service, P.O. Box 236, Thornton Road, Croydon, Surrey CR9 3RU, England.

*Please note: READERS IN SOUTH AFRICA please write to: Mills & Boon Ltd., P.O. Box 1872, Johannesburg 2000, S. Africa.

Please send me details of the Mills & Boon Subscription Scheme.

NAME (Mrs/Miss) _____ EP3

ADDRESS _____

_____

COUNTY/COUNTRY _____ POST/ZIP CODE _____

BLOCK LETTERS, PLEASE

Mills & Boon
the rose of romance